New York Times bestselling author **Anne Mather** has written since she was seven, but it was only when her first child was born that she fulfilled her dream of becoming a writer. Her first book, *Caroline*, appeared in 1966. It met with immediate success, and since then Anne has written more than 150 novels, reaching a readership which spans the world. Born and raised in the north of England, Anne still makes her home there, with her husband, two children and now grandchildren. Asked if she finds writing a lonely occupation, she replies that her characters always keep her company. In fact she is so busy sorting out their lives that she often doesn't have time for her own! An avid reader herself, she devours everything from sagas and romances to mainstream fiction and suspense.

CHAPTER ONE

HELEN was standing at the rail when the ferry docked in Santoros. Milos could see her clearly, despite the roiling tension in his gut. And he had to admit, she was still one of the most beautiful women he'd ever seen.

Or slept with, he appended, trying to make light of the fact that he was meeting her again. Although it was over fourteen years since he'd had anything to do with her, there was no denying his jumping nerves or the seething emotions just the sight of her inspired.

Theos, what was wrong with him? She'd been a wife, a mother, and a widow since that mindless interlude in London. He should be long over her—and he was, he assured himself fiercely.

Was it his imagination, or did Helen look a little harassed after her journey? Two plane flights and a ferry ride at the end of it could do that to you, he guessed. But he had no firsthand experience.

He'd been spoilt by private planes and helicopters and fast, turbo-driven yachts.

Still, she was here now and Sam—her father—would be delighted. He'd talked of little else since she'd accepted his invitation. Milos had been sure Sam would want to meet her himself, but he'd asked Milos to do it. He'd assumed their previous association would give Milos a lever he didn't have.

If he only knew!

But Sam was naturally anxious about the visit. It was almost sixteen years since he'd last seen his daughter. And then under less than favourable circumstances. According to him, his first wife had ensured that their daughter only heard one side of the story. A story that entailed a disillusioned Sam getting involved with and subsequently marrying a darkly attractive Greek woman he'd met on a business trip to Athens.

When Milos had met Helen some twenty months later she'd been no less hostile towards her father then than when she'd first discovered he'd been unfaithful to her mother. She'd blamed him. She'd been young and idealistic and impossibly naïve.

But so vulnerable, Milos reflected with unwilling honesty. And he'd taken advantage of that vulnerability. Not for her father's sake, but for his own ends. *Endaxi*, it hadn't been all his fault, he defended himself impatiently. She'd been more than willing to satisfy his demands.

The guilt had come later, of course. When he'd gone back to Greece. He'd told no one what had happened during his trip. Not his own family; not Maya, Sam's second wife; and most particularly not Sam, who had trusted him. But the worst feeling of all was that somehow he'd betrayed himself.

He scowled now, watching as the ferry's captain eased his vessel up to the quay. The trouble was, his own marriage—the marriage his father had arranged against his will—had been breaking up at that time and he'd been looking for a diversion. Helen had certainly provided that, he thought bitterly. And then she'd run out on him proving what an immature creature she was.

Naturally, he'd never expected to be in the position he was in now. Helen's alienation from her father and Maya had foolishly persuaded him that there would be no reconciliation in this lifetime. How wrong he'd been. He'd been stunned when Sam had announced that Helen and her daughter were coming to the island for a holiday. But, Helen's own husband had been killed almost a year ago, Sam had explained, and the letter he'd written expressing his condolences had apparently gone a long way to mending the rift between them.

A more cynical man might wonder if Sam's amazing change of fortune had had anything to do with his daughter's change of heart. Despite the fact that his background as a wine importer in England had had little to do with the actual cultivation of the grapes, meeting Maya and subsequently taking over her family's failing vineyard had made him a wealthy man. During the past ten years, *Ambeli Kouros*, as the vineyard was known, had gone from strength to strength and Sam Campbell had become a much respected man on the island.

A girl appeared as the ferry was docking, pushing her way through the crowd of passengers to join Helen at the rail. Not her daughter, he assured himself, despite their apparent familiarity. In a black tee shirt with some logo sprawled across the front and baggy black jeans that pooled around her ankles, she was the type of visitor Milos thought the island could well do without. Black lipstick, hair sprayed a lurid shade of green, a semi-circle of piercings etching her ears, she was as different from Helen as it was possible to be.

Skata, he thought, waiting for her to be claimed by the group of backpack-toting teenagers that were hustling to disembark. This was one of those occasions when he wished his family owned the whole island and not just a large part of it.

A wooden gangplank was run out from the quay and as the passengers moved towards it Milos saw the girl speak to Helen. He couldn't make out what she said, of course, but it appeared it wasn't something Helen wanted to hear. There was a brief heated exchange and then they both joined the rapidly decreasing exodus.

Milos blew out a breath. No, he told himself shortly. He was prepared to accept that travelling could promote the most unlikely friendships and that creature could not be Helen's daughter.

Whatever, they were coming down the gangplank now and his eyes were irresistibly drawn to Helen's flushed face. Was she hot? he wondered. Certainly, the skirt and jacket she was wearing were unsuitable attire for this climate. But was that the only reason she looked so distrait?

She'd cut her hair, he noticed, with a pang he quickly suppressed. But she was still as slim and lovely as ever. Would she recognise him? It had been over fourteen years, after all. Was he flattering himself in thinking she might remember him as well as he remembered her?

And then their eyes met and held, and the breath he'd hardly been aware he was holding got caught somewhere in the back of his throat. *Theos*, she remembered him all right. Why else would there be such a mixture of fear and loathing in her eyes?

'Who's that?'

Without her being aware of it, Melissa had noticed her distraction, and Helen managed to drag her eyes away from Milos's and say with admirable restraint, 'Who's who?'

'That man,' said Melissa flatly, hauling her backpack higher on her shoulder. 'Come on, Mum. He's staring at us. He's not your dad, is he?'

Helen gave a nervous little laugh. 'Hardly,' she said, acknowledging that only she could know the irony of that statement. 'His name's Milos Stephanides. Your grandfather must have sent him to meet us.'

'Yeah?' Melissa arched dark brows that were so exactly like her father's that Helen felt a momentary pang. 'So how do you know him?'

'Oh…' This was not a conversation Helen wanted to be having right now. 'I met him—years ago. Your grandfather asked him to look us up when he was on a visit to England.' She moistened her dry lips. 'That—that was before you were born, of course.'

'And he still remembers you?' Melissa reflected consideringly. 'What happened? Don't tell me my stiff-assed mother actually had a thing for a sexy Greek labourer!'

'No!' Helen was horrified, glancing about her to make sure no one else had heard her daughter's coarse words. 'And as far as I know, he's not a labourer. He just works for your grandfather, that's all.'

'Well, what else is there to do on a farm?' asked Melissa impatiently, and Helen sighed.

'It's not a farm.'

'Yeah, right.' Melissa gave her a sardonic look. 'You're not going to tell me.' She snorted. 'I should have had more sense than to ask.'

Helen had no time to answer that. They'd reached the stone quay and Milos was coming towards them. He was wearing a loose-fitting shirt, open halfway down his chest, she noticed, and black chinos that hugged his narrow hips and only hinted at the power of his long legs. He looked good, she thought uneasily. Dear God, it was devastating how good he looked. Cool and dark—was his hair a little longer than she remembered? But so horribly familiar, his lean handsome face the one that had haunted her dreams for all these years.

She badly wanted to turn tail and get back on the ferry. She'd known all along it was a risk coming here, but how had she been supposed to know that his would be the first face she'd see? But with Melissa breathing down her neck and her pull-along suitcase nudging at her heels, there was no alternative but to go on. She had to go through with this, she told herself. If only to prove to this smug, unsmiling stranger that she'd got over him and made herself a life.

It didn't help that in spite of her high heels—heels she'd worn in a futile attempt to boost her morale—she still had to tilt her head to look up at him. It reminded her too painfully of the past and for a moment she thought she wasn't going to be able to do this. But then sanity returned, and with admirable control she said, 'Hello, Milos. How kind of you to come and meet us. Did my father send you?'

The dig was unmistakable, but he was unperturbed by it. 'No one *sent* me,' he said, revealing the faint trace of accent she remembered so well. 'I am not an item of mail.'

Helen's lips tightened. No, you're not, she wanted to say grimly. You're far more dangerous. But all she actually said was, 'You know what I mean.' Her eyes flicked to his and swiftly away again. 'Is my father with you?'

'No.' Milos negated that hope with a cool arrogance. 'Did you have a good journey?'

'You have got to be kidding!'

It was Melissa who answered him and Helen saw Milos's eyes move beyond the girl without even acknowledging she'd spoken. 'Your daughter?' he said thinly. 'I thought she was coming with you.'

'I'm her daughter,' announced Melissa shortly, clearly resenting his attitude. 'Who're you? My grandfather's chauffeur?'

Milos's expression didn't change, but Helen was aware of the sudden withdrawal that stiffened his lean, muscular frame. 'No, yours,' he responded, without turning a hair. 'Is this all the luggage you have?'

Helen resented it, but she felt uncomfortable

now. It was bad enough having to deal with a man she had once made a fool of herself over without having to feel ashamed of her daughter's attitude.

So, 'Yes,' she said, giving Melissa a killing look. 'Is—is it far to Aghios Petros?'

'Not very,' Milos replied, taking possession of her suitcase. 'Follow me.'

'Shouldn't you say *ilthateh sto Santoros*?' asked Melissa, undaunted by her mother's embarrassment. 'That's welcome to Santoros,' she added, for Helen's benefit. 'Good, eh?'

Milos glanced at her, but if she'd expected an angry reaction, she was disappointed. 'I am pleased you're keen to learn my language,' he said smoothly. *'Then to ixera.'*

'Yeah.' But Melissa was nonplussed now, and, shoving the phrase book she'd pulled out of her backpack into the pocket of her jeans, she adopted her usual belligerence when faced with opposition of any kind. 'Well, I'm not really interested in learning Greek,' she said rudely. She glanced about her. 'Come on. Can we get moving? I need to pee.'

Helen clenched her teeth. Melissa was impossible and she saw that Milos had noticed how pushing the phrase book into her pocket had exposed a generous wedge of olive skin between her waist-band and her cropped tee shirt. It had also exposed the navel ring that they'd had a row about just the night before and she dreaded to think what kind of a mother he must believe her to be.

The quay had virtually emptied while they were talking and only the porters unloading supplies from the hold of the vessel were still working in the hot sun. Helen wished she were just wearing a vest instead of the heavy blazer, but she'd had no idea it would be so hot.

As if taking pity on her, Milos spoke again. 'Your father can't wait to see you,' he said. Then, with a careless gesture, 'My car is over here.'

'I'm looking forward to seeing him, too,' Helen confessed, keeping pace with him with some difficulty. 'Is he very ill?'

Milos halted then and gave her a stunned look. 'He's—as well as can be expected,' he said, after a moment. 'For his age, that is.' He paused and then added stiffly, 'I was sorry to hear about your husband's accident.'

'Yes.' But Helen didn't want to talk about Richard. Particularly not to him. She strove for something else to say and found the perfect response. 'How is your wife these days?'

Milos's jaw hardened. 'We are divorced,' he said tersely, obviously resenting her question just as much as she'd resented his. 'Your—husband must have been very young when he died.'

'He was—'

"Course, he was stoned at the time,' put in Melissa, apparently growing tired of being ignored. Then, before either of the adults could respond, 'Wow, are these your wheels? Cool!'

Helen met Milos's eyes without really being able to stop herself. She could almost see what he was thinking. He was wondering what kind of genes had spawned such a monster, and she couldn't blame him. She couldn't even blame it on Richard's premature demise. Melissa had been out of control long before then.

Making no response, Milos swung open the door of the sleek Mercedes before saying tersely to the girl, 'Get in the back.'

There was an unmistakable edge to his voice and predictably Melissa responded to it. 'Who are you talking to?' she demanded, making no effort to do as he'd asked. She propped her hip against the car and ran a black-lacquered nail over the gleaming silver paintwork. 'You can't tell me what to do, Milos. I'm not your daughter.'

A look of savagery crossed Milos's face at that moment and Helen guessed he was thinking that no daughter of his would ever act like this. If he only knew, she thought, unaware she had let anything of her feelings show in her face until he threw her an uncomprehending look. But, 'Just do it!' was all he said, daring Melissa to argue with him again, and, with a muffled swear word, Melissa straightened from her lounging position.

'Please,' Helen appended, dreading another scene. 'Melissa, please!'

'Oh—all right.'

Melissa sniffed, but finally she gave in. Forcing the front seat forward, she flung her backpack onto the soft Moroccan leather and climbed in after it. But she made no attempt to keep her scuffed trainers from scraping across the back of the seats in front and Helen's teeth were on edge by the time she'd settled down.

'Happy now?'

Helen was far from happy, but this wasn't the time to voice it. She was too aware of the dangers Milos represented, and of her own pitiable ability to keep the truth from him. The day had started badly, after that sleepless night on the ferry, and it had suddenly got a whole lot worse.

She got into the car when Milos indicated that she should, but she noticed that he was far from relaxed when he flung open his door and got in beside her. What was he thinking? she fretted. Had he seen anything in Melissa's face, in her words, to give him pause? Oh, God, what was she going to do if he had?

Her skirt had ridden up her thighs as she got into the vehicle and she concentrated on pulling it down as Milos thrust the car into drive and depressed the accelerator. But she couldn't help being aware of him beside her, of his lean strength coiled behind the wheel, of his long fingers on the controls. Long fingers that had once…

'I'm gonna have a car like this when I'm older,' declared Melissa from the back seat, and Helen wondered if she'd sensed the tension between them.

'You'll have to do some work first,' she said, anything to distract herself. 'Cars like this cost money.'

'I could always find myself a rich husband,' remarked her daughter irrepressibly. 'Even one who's more than twice my age.'

Helen sucked in a breath. But she refused to let herself be drawn by Melissa's unsubtle reference to her employer. 'Do—er—do you live at Aghios Petros, too?' she asked, addressing Milos, and, although she sensed his reluctance, he was forced to look her way.

'I live—not too far from there,' he replied at last. 'But I don't spend all the year on Santoros. I also have a home in Athens.'

'You do?' Helen was surprised. If he did work for her father, he was evidently paid very well.

'My family isn't involved in winemaking,' he told her flatly, successfully shattering her preconceived ideas about him. 'My father owns—ships.'

'Ships?' It was Melissa who broke in again. 'What? Like that leaky old crate that brought us from Crete?'

'Melissa!'

Helen cast another impatient look at her daughter, but Milos had apparently had enough of her insolence. 'No,' he said harshly. 'Not ferry boats, *thespinis*.' He emphasised the word. 'Tankers. Oil-tankers. Regrettably, I am one of those rich old men you spoke of so scornfully a few minutes ago.'

CHAPTER TWO

THE villa stood on a rise above terraced slopes burgeoning with green vines. A long drive wound between cypress and olive trees, with the flowering blooms of tamarisk bushes edging the road. It was a fairly large dwelling with hanging eaves, overgrown with flowering vines and bougainvillea.

'Is this it?'

Melissa was leaning forward now, her elbow digging into the back of her mother's neck, and Milos wondered what the hell Sam would make of his granddaughter. She was obviously going to be nothing like he'd expected.

'Mum!'

Helen had said nothing and Melissa prompted her to speak. 'I think this must be your grandfather's house,' she said, glancing sideways at Milos. 'Those are vineyards, aren't they?'

'*Ineh*—they are,' he agreed. 'This is the *Ambeli Kouras*.'

'Ambeli Kouros?' Once again, Melissa had to have her say. 'What the hell is that?'

'Melissa!'

Helen tried to restrain her, but Milos decided she was wasting her time. 'It means the Kouros vineyard,' he told her patiently. 'Kouros was your grandfather's wife's family name. When he took over, he retained it.'

Melissa was reflective for a moment. 'My grandfather's wife,' she said at last. 'That would be *that evil bitch Maya*, right?'

'For goodness' sake, Melissa—'

Helen was obviously horrified, but Milos recognised Helen's mother's voice in that description. 'That's right,' he said. 'So be warned. Maya doesn't take any prisoners.'

Melissa huffed, but she sat back on her seat, clearly disappointed she hadn't aroused a more explosive reaction. Helen felt obliged to intervene. 'I'm afraid Maya's name isn't particularly welcome in my family,' she said. 'I have to admit, my mother didn't want me to come.'

So, what's new? thought Milos drily. Sheila Campbell hadn't liked him either. 'I expect she doesn't trust Sam,' he ventured mildly. 'Either

that, or she thinks it's too soon for you to be thinking of starting over.'

'You mean, since Richard died?' Helen queried,
her lips folding together in a thin line. 'No. She—
er—she's of the opinion that I should get married
again.' And he could make what he liked of that!
she seemed to add silently.

'Yeah, she wants Mum to marry a wrinkly,' put
in Melissa, before Milos could make any comment. Which was just as well. Helen's statement
had thrown him for six. 'Mark Greenaway. He
must be sixty if he's a day. Like I'd want him for
a *daddy*!'

Helen caught her breath. 'Mark is not a wrinkly,' she protested hotly. 'And he's nowhere near
sixty.' She cast Milos an awkward glance. 'He's
my boss. He owns an engineering company and
I'm his personal assistant.'

'Really?' Milos managed to sound only margin-
ally interested. 'Does he have family, too?'

'If you mean, is he married, then no,' said Helen
stiffly. 'He's a widower, without any children of
his own.'

'Oh, bliss!' muttered Melissa contemptuously.
'The man's a wimp and you know it. If it wasn't

for the fact that Dad never did any work, you'd never have considered taking a job with him.'

'That's not true!'

Helen was embarrassed, and Milos wondered how she could let her daughter get away with saying what she did. It was as if Helen was scared of what Melissa might do next, and, judging by the girl's attitude, she might have a point.

Suddenly aware that he was staring at her, Milos dragged his eyes away. Was it only nervousness that was stopping her from making any attempt to get out of the car, or was there something else she wanted to say?

His stomach tightened, but before he could identify the reason Melissa broke the uneasy silence that had fallen. 'Well, duh—are we getting out or what?' she asked, and Milos steeled his expression and swung open his door.

By the time he'd circled the car, Helen had got out, too, her long legs, in the ridiculously high heels, attracting his unwilling gaze. *'Iseh kala?'* he probed. 'Are you okay?'

There'd been a reluctant concern in his voice and she responded to it. Though not in the way he'd anticipated. 'Do you care?' she exclaimed, exposing her real feelings for the first time. 'Do you care about anyone but yourself? Forget it, Milos. It's too late to pretend you have a conscience now.'

Milos's jaw dropped, but the angry retort that sprang to his lips was stifled by the sight of Melissa clambering over the seats to the front of the car.

'Do you mind?' she demanded as he stared at her now instead of her mother. 'I want to get out. You're in the way.'

Milos was too stunned by the way she was trashing his vehicle to do anything but reach for Helen's hand with the intention of drawing her aside so that the girl could open the door.

But he'd acted without thinking, and before his fingertips could register the silky feel of her skin or the palpitating pulse at her wrist Helen had yanked her arm away, rubbing her hand as if he'd contaminated her.

'Don't—don't touch me!' she said accusingly, and for once he was grateful to Melissa's overloud, 'Thanks a bunch!' for drowning out her mother's choked words.

They'd been given rooms at the back of the villa. Pale tiled floors, high ceilings, and lots of dark wood furniture, contrasting their coolness with the shimmering heat outside. A balcony with white painted chairs and a table invited inspection, and beyond the hillside fell away to the coastal plain.

What a view, thought Helen, cupping the back of her neck with hands that were still damp from the emotions she'd felt earlier when she'd met her father's second wife. Dealing with Milos had been hard enough, but Maya had proved another matter entirely.

It was obvious she didn't want them here. She'd made that perfectly plain, despite her almost sickening treatment of Milos. He was evidently *persona grata* at the villa. They were not, and she'd wasted no time in letting them know it.

But what had really shocked Helen was the news that her father was working. Working! When she'd imagined him wheelchair-ridden or worse. That was the impression he'd given her in his letters. That he desperately wanted to see her again before he—

Before he, what? He'd stopped short at saying he was actually dying, she remembered. He'd just let her believe he was seriously ill; that he didn't know how long he had left.

'What do you think?' Melissa had come to lean

in the doorway of her room that adjoined Helen's suite. For once, there was a look of uncertainty on her young face. 'Are we gonna stay or do we just spit in his eye and catch the next ferry out of here?'

'Melissa!' Helen spoke automatically, but her heart wasn't really in it. The girl was only voicing things she'd thought of herself. Was staying here really an option? Being brought here under false pretences didn't augur well for her future relationship with her father.

'Well, you're not exactly enthusiastic about it, are you?' Melissa countered. She nodded towards her mother's suitcase. 'You haven't even started to unpack.'

'And you have?'

Helen swung about to face her and Melissa pulled a face. 'Hey, a few tees and a spare pair of jeans don't need much unpacking. I unzip my pack, haul out my stuff, and shove it in a drawer. That's it.'

Helen's mouth compressed. 'You haven't just brought jeans and tee shirts!'

'Haven't I?'

Helen gave up. 'Have it your own way,' she said, too weary to even remember how optimistic she'd been about taking this trip. It wasn't just for her father, she acknowledged. It was for her and Melissa, too. Anything to get her daughter away from the unfavourable influences that were making life so difficult at home.

She walked towards a chest of drawers where one of the maids had left a tray of coffee and some fresh lemonade. 'D'you want a drink?'

'I guess.' Melissa regarded her wearily now, pushing herself away from the door and slouching across the room. 'What's up?'

'You have to ask?' Helen shook her head. 'Well, let's see, my daughter—my delightful daughter—has done her best to humiliate me; I discover the father I haven't seen for sixteen years has been lying to me; and his wife has made it clear she doesn't want us here. Need I go on?'

Melissa shrugged. 'Do I look like I care?'

'Oh, right.' Helen took off her jacket and pulled the hem of her cream silk top out of the waistband of her skirt and used it to fan her midriff. 'So, you'd stay?'

'Sure. Why not?'

'I've just told you that we're not wanted here.'

'So?'

'So—unlike you, I don't like confrontation.'

'Get over it, Mum.' Melissa helped herself to a glass of lemonade before continuing, 'In any case, I thought you were pretty hard on Milos. If it wasn't for him, we'd prob'ly still be standing outside in the blazing sun. Maya was in no hurry to invite us in, was she?'

'I don't need Milos Stephanides's help,' said Helen tensely, and then struggled to control herself. But the last thing she needed right now was to get into a discussion with Melissa about Milos. She was too nervous, too on edge. She might easily say something she'd regret.

Cradling the cup of coffee she'd poured herself between her palms, she moved back to the windows. Meeting him again had proved far harder than she'd ever imagined. She should have got over him by now, but she was no longer so sure she had.

And how pathetic was that?

'D'you think he and Maya are, like, doing it?' asked Melissa suddenly, her reflection appearing in the glass of the window beside her mother's, and Helen turned to give her a horrified look.

'Doing what?' she exclaimed, but she was very much afraid she knew what the child meant. Maya had been fulsomely glad to see him.

'Hey, do I need to draw you a picture?' Melissa grimaced. 'You know what I mean.'

'No.' Helen wouldn't make it easy for her. 'No, I don't.'

'Well, duh—I don't mean her and your old man, do I?'

Helen stared at her. 'You're suggesting that Milos—that Milos and Maya might be—'

'Getting it on?' finished Melissa helpfully, when her mother faltered. 'Yeah. Why not? Didn't you see the way she was all over him? Like a rash! And he's not married. He said so.'

'She is.'

'And your point is?'

Helen was emphatic. 'No.'

'Hello? Don't tell me you think your queen of a stepmother wouldn't do such a thing.' Melissa shook her head. 'Get real, Helen. It wouldn't be the first time she broke up a relationship.'

Her mother was aghast, but all she could say was, 'Don't call me Helen.'

'What do I call you, then? Dumb?' Melissa groaned. 'Mum, this guy's a babe magnet. Just 'cos Maya's already got a husband doesn't mean she can't have a bit on the side as well.'

'Melissa!' Helen nearly choked on her coffee. 'You appal me, you really do.'

The girl shrugged. 'Well, don't say I didn't warn you.'

Helen gasped. 'She was pleased to see him, that's all.'

'Wasn't she just?' Melissa snorted. 'Whatever. The guy's hot. Even you must have noticed. Or have you forgotten what it's like to—?'

'That will do.' Helen couldn't listen to any more. She took a steadying breath and changed the subject. 'Is your room nice?'

'Nice?' Melissa finished the lemonade in her glass and returned it to the tray. 'You're determined not to treat me like an adult, aren't you?'

'Because you're not an adult, Melissa. You're thirteen, not twenty-three.'

'I'll be fourteen soon. Why can't you remember that?'

'Oh, I remember exactly how old you are,' said Helen with feeling. Did she ever? Then in a spirit of compromise, 'So you think we should stay?'

'Do kids have a vote?'

'Of course, you do.' Helen sighed. 'I thought you might want to meet your grandfather.'

Melissa pulled a face. 'Like I need another old man in my life!'

'So what are you saying?'

'Well, we're here, aren't we? And this place isn't bad. And our staying will definitely get up Maya's nose.'

Helen couldn't prevent the smile that tugged at her lips. 'You're impossible!'

'But you love me anyway,' said Melissa, dodging her mother's playful nudge. Then as the sound of a car accelerating up the villa reached their ears she arched a mocking brow. 'Hey, is that who I think it is?'

Helen's stomach contracted. She had no doubt that the car belonged to her father. Someone, Maya probably, had informed him of their arrival, and he'd evidently dropped whatever it was he'd been doing to return to the house.

Immediately, the prospect of unpacking, of doing as Melissa had suggested and staying here, lost its appeal. Dear God, what was she going to say to him? How many more lies was he planning to tell her? What excuse could he possibly make for hinting that he only had a short time to live?

Melissa, who had dashed out onto the balcony to try and see the new arrival, returned with a disappointed face. 'You can't see the drive from here,' she said. 'Do you think it's him?'

'If you mean, do I think it's your grandfather, then, yes, I think so,' said Helen tersely. And, as if just noticing her daughter's appearance, she added, 'Don't you have anything more suitable to wear? Shorts, for example?'

'Yeah, right. Like I'm going to dress like a dork!' Melissa was disgusted. 'And don't take your bad temper out on me. It's not my fault.'

Helen's anger subsided as quickly as it had appeared. 'I just wish you didn't always wear black!'

'It's a fashion statement,' said Melissa airily, making for the door. 'Anyway, I'm going to see what's going on downstairs. I don't want that evil bitch queering the pitch.'

'Stay where you are.' Helen moved quickly to intercept her. 'You are not leaving this room on your own.' She took a deep breath. 'And watch your language where your grandfather's wife is concerned. Stop trying to be a poor imitation of your grandmother.'

Melissa's cheeks turned a little pink. 'I don't know why you're defending her,' she muttered. 'She ruined your life, didn't she?'

'Maybe.' Helen wasn't prepared to argue the

point. Then, giving in, 'Oh, give me a minute
to use the bathroom and we'll both go and get it
over with.'

Melissa frowned. 'You're really not looking forward to this, are you?'

'No, I'm really not.'

'Because your old man snowed you?'

'Because he lied to me, yes.' Helen hadn't the
energy to go any further. She picked up her hand-
bag and rummaged for her comb. 'Do I look all
right?'

Melissa gave her a grudging once-over. 'Not
bad for an older woman,' she conceded. 'Milos
thinks you're cool, anyway.'

Helen flushed. 'Oh, right,' she said, even though
the girl's words had given her a cheap forbidden
thrill. 'Let's go before I lose my nerve.'

CHAPTER THREE

BEFORE Helen could reach for the door handle, however, someone knocked from outside, and her stomach took a nosedive.

'Who is it?' she called faintly, but Melissa simply took the initiative and opened the door.

The man who stood outside was instantly recognisable. Tall and lean, with gaunt features and thick grey-streaked sandy hair, her father looked almost as apprehensive as she did. 'Helen,' he said thickly, making no attempt to step into the room. 'Dammit, I should have gone to meet you myself, instead of getting Milos to do it. I've waited so long for this moment. Can you forgive me for being scared I'd f—mess it up?'

Helen couldn't move. Now that he was here, actually standing in front of her, all the years between them seemed like so much wasted space.

'Well, say something,' he exclaimed raggedly, and she realised he'd mistaken her silence for withdrawal.

As if growing impatient with both of them, Melissa stepped forward. 'Hi,' she said, regarding him with critical dark eyes. 'I'm Melissa Shaw; your granddaughter.' She paused, glancing at Helen. 'Don't mind Mum. She's having a hard time remembering who you are.'

'That's not true,' began Helen quickly, desperate not to antagonise him before they'd had a chance to get to know one another again.

But Sam Campbell didn't let her finish. 'I wouldn't blame her if she was,' he said gruffly. 'Goodness knows, I'm not proud of the way I've let things drift.' He took a breath. 'It's so good to see you again—to see *both* of you. I've been a fool to let Sheila call the shots all these years.'

Helen hesitated. 'It's not all your fault,' she said, ignoring the rolling-eyed look Melissa gave her. 'I was too stubborn, I guess. I wasn't prepared to listen to you.'

'And now you are?'

Helen made a helpless gesture. 'I'm—older,' she said obliquely. And then, because she couldn't ignore the reasons that had brought her here, 'When you said you were ill…'

Hectic colour flooded his cheeks. 'That wasn't true—'

'I know that now.'

'Milos told you?'

'No. Maya.' Helen saw the way his mouth tightened at the news. 'I don't think she wants us here.'

Sam shook his head, his impatience evident now. 'It's not her call,' he said. 'This is my house, not hers.' He pushed nervous hands deep into the pockets of his cotton trousers. 'I have to ask: does my deception make a difference?'

Helen lifted slim shoulders. 'It does, of course. But I don't know how I feel.' She saw Melissa watching her and went on carefully, 'Perhaps we ought to take one day at a time.'

'Would you have come if I hadn't pretended to be ill?' he demanded fiercely and Helen had to admit that the answer was probably no. And, as if he was able to read her thoughts, he went on, 'So now you know why I did it.'

'I suppose so.'

He took a deep breath then, glancing up and down the hall outside. 'Look,' he said. 'I'm sure you're tired. You'd like a rest.' He frowned. 'Have you had anything to eat?'

'We had some coffee.'

'But nothing to eat?' Her father nodded and glanced at his watch. 'Okay. It's nearly half past ten. Why don't I have Sofia bring you some rolls and some fresh coffee? Then you can relax until lunchtime.'

'That sounds good to me.' Helen glanced at Melissa. 'What do you think?'

'Well, I don't want to rest,' said Melissa with her usual perversity. She looked at her grandfather. 'Can't I go with you?'

'Melissa!'

Helen was about to object when Sam Campbell said, 'Why not?' A smile warmed his rather austere features. 'If your mother doesn't mind.'

Helen could think of no reason why Melissa shouldn't go with him. 'Um—no,' she murmured. And then another thought occurred to her. 'Is Milos still here?'

Melissa rolled her eyes again at this, but thankfully her grandfather didn't see her. 'No, he's gone,' he said, suddenly more cheerful. 'Okay, Melissa, I'll give you the guided tour, eh? And introduce you to Alex.'

'Alex?'

Both Helen and her daughter spoke in unison and once again a momentary hesitation crossed his face. 'Alex. Alex Campbell,' he said with some reluctance. 'Maya's son.'

* * *

Melissa came back before lunch, full of herself and of the things she'd seen.

'This is some place, Mum,' she exclaimed, flinging herself onto Helen's bed with a complete disregard for the silk coverlet. 'Did you know they make wine here as well as grow the grapes?'

Helen hadn't known that but she was quite content to let Melissa tell her all about it. Having spent the morning unpacking both her suitcase and Melissa's backpack and taking a shower, she felt much more optimistic about the trip. If it helped to show her daughter there was more to life than skipping school and hanging about on street corners with kids whose main pastimes were smoking pot and shoplifting, she'd be more than happy.

A vain hope, perhaps, but at least it was a beginning and Melissa seemed to have enjoyed herself.

'He took me down to the mill,' she said, tugging on the rings that circled her ear with a careless finger. 'It was good. He let me taste some of the wine they'd made last year.'

'Really?' Helen restrained herself from saying that drinking wine at her age and at this hour of the morning wasn't very sensible. 'So what was it like?'

'The wine? Okay, I guess.' Melissa didn't sound impressed. 'I don't think I'm going to be an alcoholic.'

Helen breathed a little easier. 'That's a relief.'

'Why?' Melissa looked at her from beneath lowered lids. 'Are you afraid I'm gonna take after Richard?'

'No.'

'Good.' Melissa looked as if she wanted to say something more and then thought better of it. 'Anyway, Sam treats me like my opinion matters. I like that.'

I bet, thought Helen, but all she said was, 'Did he tell you to call him Sam?'

'No.' Now Melissa pouted a bit. 'But I can't call him Granddad, can I?'

Helen acknowledged that might be a stretch. 'I guess not. So—did you meet Alex?'

'Oh, sure.' Melissa was annoyingly casual. 'But to begin with, I had some breakfast. He was going to take me on a tour of the house,' she added, 'but Maya kept complaining we were getting in her way, so we got in the Jeep and went down to the mill.'

'I see.'

'That's when I met Alex.' Melissa's lips quirked. 'He's cool.'

Cool? Helen couldn't help herself. She was curious. 'You liked him?'

'What's not to like? At least he was friendly.'

'He speaks English?'

'Yeah.'

'So—how old is he?'

Melissa was deliberately obtuse. 'Older than me.'

'Melissa!'

'Oh, okay.' Melissa rumpled her hair. 'He's not your brother, if that's what's worrying you. He's twenty-six. Maya was like you. She was only seventeen when Alex was born.'

It was a couple of days later when Milos decided to check up on Sam's house guests.

It wasn't anything to do with him, he knew, but something drew him back to the vineyard. It was easy to tell himself that, as he'd collected them from the ferry, he felt some responsibility for their well being. But the truth was, Helen and her unlikely daughter intrigued him. He wanted to know more about them. He wanted to know more about *her*.

Sam was having a late breakfast when he arrived. Milos guessed his friend had already been down to the winery to check on developments there, and now he was enjoying a lazy repast, seated at the table that had been laid in the shade of a clump of lemon trees.

'Milos,' he exclaimed, when the younger man emerged from the shadows of the villa. 'This is an unexpected pleasure. Will you join me?'

'For coffee, only,' said Milos, shaking the other man's hand and urging him to resume his seat. 'I was—passing, and I thought I might enquire how your daughter and granddaughter are enjoying their holiday.'

'Oh...' Sam pulled a wry face. 'Well, I think Helen is glad of the break. She's had a pretty tough time since her husband was killed. Richard—well, Richard seems to have been a bit of a waster, if you ask me. Why else would Helen have had to give up her own home and move back in with her mother unless money was tight?'

Milos wasn't sure he wanted to hear this. Talking about the man who had lived with Helen all those years aroused mixed emotions inside him. It wasn't that he was jealous, he assured himself. How could you be jealous of a dead man? But the fact remained, he didn't like the sound of Richard either. Was he the reason Melissa was so obviously out of control?

Maya emerged from the house at that moment and both men rose automatically to their feet. A swarthy, attractive woman in her early forties, she was of medium height, but rather generously proportioned. She tended to wear long flowing skirts that disguised her figure, yet the blouse she'd chosen revealed a liberal amount of cleavage. She was a distant cousin of Milos's mother, and she never let him forget that they were related.

'I thought I heard voices,' she exclaimed, coming towards them and reaching up to bestow a wet kiss on Milos's cheek. She spoke in her own language, which she much preferred to English. 'I didn't know you were here, Milos,' she went on reprovingly. 'Sam, haven't you offered our guest some refreshment?'

'I have, and he only wants coffee,' replied Sam, sinking back into his own chair. 'Perhaps you'd ask Sofia to fetch some, Maya? This pot is definitely getting cold.'

Maya's lips tightened. 'Just call and she'll come, Samuel,' she retorted impatiently. 'She has little enough to do, goodness knows.' She turned to

Milos again. 'It's so good to see you.' She tapped his arm in a playful gesture. 'You don't visit half often enough.'

Milos managed a polite disclaimer, but he was beginning to think he'd made a mistake in coming here. He doubted Maya would approve of his reasons for doing so. She'd made her feelings very plain the morning Helen and her daughter had arrived. And Helen herself was unlikely to be glad to see him. He remembered the tension that had been there between them on that drive up from the harbour.

'He's come to see Helen,' Sam put in then, settling the matter. 'Where is she, Maya? I haven't seen her this morning.'

'That's because she doesn't get up as early as we do,' declared Maya crisply. She turned a smiling face to Milos again. 'Will you stay for lunch?'

'Oh, I don't—' Milos was beginning when Helen herself appeared from around the side of the villa, and Sam rose eagerly to his feet.

'Well, here she is,' he exclaimed, reverting at once to English. He went to meet his daughter with evident pleasure. 'We thought you weren't up yet.'

'Did you?'

Helen had a smile for her father, but then her eyes moved beyond him to where Milos and Maya were standing together. Her lips tightened, as if she'd attributed that misapprehension jointly to both of them, and Milos felt his own instinctive rejection of her assumption.

Struggling to remember why he was here, he managed a polite, *'Kalimera,'* separating himself from his cousin almost involuntarily. 'How are you?'

Helen took a visible breath. 'I'm fine, thank you,' she said, the slim hand she used to check the upswept pony-tail at the back of her head revealing a nervousness she was trying hard not to show.

But Milos noticed. Noticed, too, that in a sleeveless top and navy shorts she looked younger, less on edge. The sun had already touched her skin with a rosy glow, and, although he suspected the hectic colour in her cheeks owed more to her mood than the climate, it suited her.

'Kala,' he said now. 'Good.'

'Milos wondered how you were settling in.'

Once again Sam chose to move the conversation on, and Milos saw the way she responded to this news. It was hardly flattering.

'Really?' she said, as if she didn't believe him, and Maya clicked her tongue.

'Greek men are sometimes too considerate for their own good,' she remarked pointedly, and Helen gave her stepmother a studied look.

'Do you think so?' she remarked casually, and Milos realised she'd already got Maya's measure.

'I think so?' said Maya shortly, and although Milos had sympathised with Helen's attitude her words caught him on the raw. Dammit, they'd been lovers. She was acting as if they were total strangers.

'Have you been for a walk?' asked Sam, not allowing the hostility between the two women to deter him, and Helen turned back to her father with another warm smile.

'I was just in the garden,' she said. 'There are so many exotic flowers here and Melissa was showing me the fountain.'

'Melissa's with you?' Sam looked back the way she'd come. 'Where is she?'

'Poking her nose where it is not wanted, I expect,' murmured Maya, barely audibly, but Helen's ears were sharp.

'I think we're all guilty of that at times, don't you?' she countered, before turning back to her father. 'She'll be along presently. She's discovered a litter of kittens behind a water barrel and she's absolutely entranced.'

'Ugh!' Maya shuddered. 'Well, I hope she does not attempt to bring any of them into the villa.'

'She won't,' said Sam impatiently, but he looked to his daughter for confirmation.

'I hope not,' she agreed, but Milos saw the way her lips twitched in sudden amusement at the thought.

Her lower lip was fuller than her upper one, and Milos knew an almost feral urge to brush his thumb across its plump contours. Relaxed, as it was now, her mouth was incredibly soft and sexy, and with amazement he found how easy it was to recall how sensuous it had felt beneath his...

Skata!

'I think perhaps I ought to be going,' he said abruptly, and both Sam and Maya showed their surprise.

'But you haven't had coffee,' protested Sam at once, walking to the villa door and summoning the maidservant. 'Coffee for my guests, Sofia,' he ordered when she appeared, and Milos was obliged to accept that he couldn't walk out now.

'Look, I have to go back to the mill for a while,'

his host continued, 'but Helen will look after you, won't you, my dear?' And, without giving her a chance to reply, 'Come along, Maya. I have something I want to discuss with you.'

In a matter of minutes, they were alone, but Helen made no attempt to sit down. A pregnant silence, broken only by the clicking of the cicadas, enveloped them until Sofia appeared again with the requested refreshments.

She set the tray on the table and then departed again and Milos decided he had been ignored long enough.

'Do you want coffee?' he asked, and Helen, who had been standing some distance away from him, staring at the view, gave him a careless glance over her shoulder.

'No, thanks.'

Milos's jaw tightened, but he was determined not to give her any reason to walk out on him. 'As you wish,' he said, strolling across the paved terrace towards her. 'It will give us more time to get to know one another again.'

Helen's expression was not encouraging. 'I don't think so,' she said. 'Why don't you just get in your very expensive car and go away? I won't tell my father if you don't.'

Milos suppressed the angry response that rose to his lips. 'Why would I do that?' he inquired instead. 'Your father would like us to be friends.'

Helen snorted. 'My father doesn't know you as I do.'

'I'll give you that.' Milos refused to be provoked. 'I'm not in the habit of sleeping with members of my own sex.'

'You surprise me.' She was deliberately insolent. 'From what I've read, men like you are more than willing to try every—ouch!'

She didn't get the chance to finish what she was saying. She had just stepped beyond the point of no return and Milos's hand shot out and gripped the soft flesh of her arm just above her elbow. He jerked her towards him with little care for her sensibilities, enjoying the brief sense of power it gave him.

'What is it with you?' he demanded, anger thickening his voice. 'We both know that what happened between us all those years ago wasn't exactly unexpected. And what was it, after all?' he added as a disturbing drift of her flowery fragrance invaded his nostrils, briefly making him forget what he'd been going to say. 'We had sex. Pretty good sex, as I recall, but so what? It's what men and women do when they're attracted to one another.'

'Women from your background,' she retorted, not prepared to give in even though he was sure he must be hurting her. He was hurting himself, for God's sake, but in an entirely different way. 'I'm not like you.'

'Oh, but you are,' he countered harshly. 'Whatever that—youth you married was like, when we were together you didn't care who I was.'

'That was because I didn't know who you were,' she exclaimed. 'And don't—don't speak about Richard. He—he was a decent man.'

'That's not what your daughter says,' Milos taunted recklessly. 'As far as I can gather, he definitely had faults of his own. Why did you marry him, Helen? Did you really love him? Or was it just to stop your mother from finding out what a promiscuous creature you'd turned out to be?'

'You bastard!'

She wanted to strike him then. For a heart-stopping moment, she stared at him, and although the hostility between them was palpable there were other, less-identifiable emotions swirling in the violet depths of her eyes. She tried to jerk back, but she didn't make it, and the raging heat of her body against his sent the blood rushing to his groin.

'Did you really believe we could be indifferent to each other?' he asked thickly, aware of a violent desire to kiss her, to pull the quivering curve of her thighs even closer to his aching shaft. This wasn't meant to happen, the voice of sanity warned him, but right then he was deaf to everything but his own urgent needs.

'Hey—what's going on?'

The child's voice provided the necessary draught of cool air to bring him to his senses. His hand dropped instantly to his side and he stepped back on legs that were almost as unsteady as Helen's own.

'Melissa,' he said, and he was amazed to hear how controlled he sounded in the circumstances. 'Um—your mother had something in her eye. I was just trying to get it out.'

CHAPTER FOUR

MILOS was persuaded to stay for lunch, after all.

Helen had been hoping he would go so that she could sort out her chaotic feelings. But with Melissa adding her support to Maya's renewed invitation, for some reason Milos had acquiesced.

Helen dared not wonder why. He was a devil, she thought, viewing her flushed face in the bathroom mirror. She'd sought refuge in her own suite of rooms, leaving Melissa and Maya to entertain their visitor, desperate to avoid another destructive altercation with him.

But she knew that sooner or later she had to go down again and behave as if nothing had happened. As it was, leaving Melissa with him had been a calculated risk. Who knew what her daughter might say if she was asked personal questions about the man she believed to be her father? After the way she'd spoken in the car, it was obvious she retained little respect for Richard.

However, what worried Helen most was her

own unwelcome response to Milos. She'd never dreamt he might behave as he had, or that what had begun as a childish provocation should so quickly deteriorate into a mindless assault on her senses. She'd sensed he'd wanted to kiss her, and the awful thing was she'd wanted it, too. Wanted more, if she was honest.

Dear God, she must be crazy!

Lunch itself wasn't quite the ordeal Helen had anticipated. Her father joined them and Melissa seemed to be easier to manage when he was there. Not that he'd persuaded her to abandon her jeans in favour of a pair of her mother's shorts, but Helen had noticed that her daughter no longer smeared black lipstick all over her mouth whenever they left their rooms.

She was relieved, too, to find that Maya had made sure that Milos was seated between her and Sam, which negated any private conversation between her guests. Which suited Helen just fine.

Nevertheless, she was intensely conscious of Milos's dark eyes resting on her frequently throughout the meal, and, although she wasn't particularly hungry, she was grateful for the wine-glass at her fingertips, which provided at least a fragile barrier between them.

Melissa, however, was another matter, and just when Helen was beginning to think she was out of danger the girl addressed Milos directly.

'Did you come in your car?' she asked eagerly. She pushed aside the plate of beef and lamb kebabs that Maya had served with rice and salad in favour of the *loukoumades*, or deep-fried dough-nuts dipped in a honey syrup, which were much more to her liking. 'How fast can it go?'

'On this island?' Milos spoke tolerantly. 'Not very.' His eyes flickered to Helen's anxious face and away again. 'Why don't you ask your mother if she'll let you come for a drive with me and I'll show you?'

'I don't think so.' Helen disliked him putting her on the spot again. 'I—we couldn't put you out like that.'

'It's no problem,' he assured her smoothly, and Helen wanted to scream in frustration when Melissa said, 'There you are, Mum. At least some-one cares if I have some fun.'

'Oh, Melissa.' It was her grandfather who spoke now, and Helen saw the way the girl visibly wilted beneath his wounded gaze. 'And I thought you were happy here. Was I wrong?'

Melissa's pale skin turned a little pink. 'Oh—

no,' she protested, and Helen realised in amazement that she genuinely wanted to please him. 'I
mean, going out in the Jeep's okay, but it's not a
Mercedes!'

Her grandfather pulled a wry face. 'Well, that's
put me in my place, hasn't it?'

'No.' Melissa didn't realise he was teasing her.
'But Milos has offered.'

'Mr Stephanides,' corrected Helen shortly, but
her nemesis merely shook his head.

'Milos will do,' he said, with annoying complacency. 'So—what do you think, Sam? Um—
Helen?'

Maya gave an impatient exclamation. 'You
surely can't seriously be considering entertain-
ing a child, Milos,' she exclaimed. 'Sam?' She
turned to her husband. 'Am I not right?'

'I suppose it's up to Milos,' declared her husband mildly. 'Helen?'

How could she object? She could hardly say
she didn't want Milos anywhere near her daughter when she couldn't offer an explanation why.
They all thought her reservations were ones of
politeness, when in fact she lived in fear of Milos
discovering exactly who Melissa was.

'I—well—'

'That's settled, then,' said Melissa triumphantly. She looked at Milos. 'Can we do it today?'

'I don't see why not.' Milos frowned. Then he said, 'I wonder if you'd like to come to Vassilios. That's my house. There's a pool there. And horses. And you'll probably meet my sister, Rhea. She's staying at my parents' villa at the moment, but she spends more time at Vassilios because of the pool. She's actually not that much older than you are.'

'How old is she?' asked Melissa at once, and Helen's heart faltered in her chest.

'Oh—eighteen, I think,' said Milos carelessly, apparently unaware of Helen's tension. Then, before Melissa could comment on her own age, he added, 'Your mother's welcome to join us.'

Helen's relief at this reprieve was short-lived however. 'As a matter of fact, I'm hoping Helen will spend the afternoon with me,' said her father warmly. 'We haven't spent much time together since her arrival, and I'd like to show her our operation.'

In an ideal world, Helen would have been delighted to spend some time with Sam. As it was, her agreement was more obligatory than enthusiastic and Melissa went off with Milos, clearly excited at the prospect of his undiluted attention.

'She'll be all right,' her father said, after the Mercedes had driven away, and even Maya added her endorsement of that statement.

'She doesn't know how lucky she is,' she said, with the usual edge to her voice. 'Milos is a busy man. If it wasn't for the fact that he's my cousin, I doubt if he'd have put himself out.'

'I think he likes Melissa,' remarked her husband mildly, sharing a rueful smile with his daughter. 'Why not? Despite the way she dresses, she is quite a character. And he must regret not having any children of his own.'

'Did he and his wife not have any children?' asked Helen, unable to resist the question, and Maya gave a scornful snort.

'Eleni?' she said contemptuously. 'That woman wouldn't risk her figure by having children.' She shook her head. 'Milos would never have married her if it hadn't been for his father.'

'It—it wasn't a love match, then?' ventured Helen, aware that she was chancing Maya's suspicions by showing so much interest in Milos's personal affairs.

But Maya didn't seem to notice. She was enjoying herself too much. 'A love match,' she echoed. 'How naïve you are, Helen. Aristotle—

that's Milos's father—wanted a business alliance with Andreas Costas. Having his son marry Eleni Costas was just the lever he needed.'

Helen absorbed this in silence, and Sam, seeing his chance, took her arm. 'Come along, my dear,' he said. 'Unless you think it will be too hot for you. I'm afraid the Jeep doesn't have air conditioning,' he added, pulling a wry face. 'But I'm willing to leave all the windows open.'

They drove first to the winery and Sam introduced her to some of the people who worked there. He also showed her how he'd used a couple of caves, one of the natural features of the island, for storing the bottled vintage. It was deliciously cool walking along the aisles of racks filled with the vineyards' product, and Helen appreciated it.

'Right now this is a comparatively small operation,' Sam said. 'Most of the wineries on the islands only bottle their wines for local consumption. We do that, of course, but at present we're involved in talks with a supermarket chain. As yet it's not all cut and dried, but it should give us a foothold on the mainland. If it comes off, it should make a great difference to our business.'

Helen looked at him. 'You love it, don't you?'

'Being my own boss?' Sam grimaced. 'Who

wouldn't? But the best part of it all is knowing that this is my achievement. Maya's father was an alcoholic, you know, and when we came here the whole place was in a state of decay.'

'So—it wasn't a question of marrying Maya for her money?' suggested Helen carefully, and her father turned to give her a resigned look.

'Is that what your mother said?'

Helen shrugged. 'Something like that.'

'Well, it isn't true. When we got together, Maya didn't have a penny, and this place was ankle-deep in debt.'

Helen nodded, and, as if needing to explain himself, Sam went on, 'I don't know what she's told you, but Sheila and I were having problems long before Maya came on the scene. Okay, maybe I shouldn't have walked out on my family, but God knows, Helen, I never intended for us to be estranged.'

Helen said nothing, but there was too much emotion in her father's voice for her to disregard his sincerity. Divorce was an ugly word, and it often generated bitterness between the partners. She wanted to believe him. She wanted him to understand how betrayed she'd felt, too. Maybe in time they would come to a complete understanding. At least coming here had been a beginning.

As they were leaving the bottling plant they ran into Alex. Helen had met Maya's son the night before, when he'd joined the family for the evening meal, and she'd been struck by the differences between him and his mother. Whereas Maya obviously resented them coming here, making little attempt to hide the fact that she didn't approve of the deception her husband had perpetrated by pretending he was ill, Alex was easygoing and friendly. Helen had liked him at once.

'I see you're being given the grand tour,' he remarked now, exchanging a humorous look with her father. 'Is he trying to persuade you that growing grapes is a rewarding occupation?'

'You and I both know it can be the most frustrating occupation there is,' retorted Sam with some feeling. He turned to his daughter. 'Alex is grumbling because I recruited him as soon as he left college. He's become my right-hand man in recent years. I don't know what I'd do without him.'

'You'd manage,' said Alex drily, but Helen sensed there was a genuine understanding between the two men. He was the son her father had never had, she thought, wondering if that had been one of the reasons for her parents' break-up. There was no doubt that Sheila hadn't wanted any more children. Helen had heard her say as much many times.

They continued on, paying a brief call at the mill where the grapes were crushed, before entering Sam's office where the commercial arm of the business was conducted. A young computer operator brought them a bottle of wine and two glasses, and Helen was quite glad to sit down for a while. The heat really was quite intense.

They talked for a while about wine-growing and the different qualities of various grapes, and then Sam said with sudden fierceness, 'You don't know how glad I am to see you here, Helen. Can you ever forgive me for the methods I used to achieve it?'

Helen studied the wine in her glass for a moment. Then she looked up at him with rueful eyes. 'We've both been at fault,' she said. 'Me, for not being prepared to listen to reason. And you for giving up on me far too soon.'

'I sent Milos to see you,' protested her father, and Helen thought how fatalistic that had been. That one action had changed her life for ever and systematically destroyed any hopes of their reconciliation.

'Anyway, that's all in the past now,' she said, not wanting to remember the frightened child she had been. Finding herself pregnant at seventeen had been terrifying enough without her mother threatening to throw her out if she refused to marry the baby's father...

'But I want to know about your past,' persisted her father. 'I want to know about this man you married: Richard Shaw. Didn't your mother think you were too young to make such a life-changing decision?'

Helen's lips twisted. 'Not really.'

'So she was all for it?'

'She didn't object,' said Helen obliquely. 'And then, when Melissa came along...'

'Of course. Melissa.' Her father smiled. 'I think I understand now. You were going to have a baby and the decision was taken for you. Didn't your mother ever tell you that that was how she and I got together?'

'No!'

Helen was stunned. But it explained so much. Not least, the struggle her mother and father had had to make their marriage work.

'Were you happy?'

Sam's question was well-meant, she knew, but he deserved to know at least a little of the truth. 'Melissa—isn't Richard's child,' she said. 'He knew that, but he wanted to marry me anyway.'

'And why not?' Sam was endearingly defensive, and Helen thought how different her life might have been if he'd been there to support her. 'You're a beautiful woman, my dear. Any man would be proud to call you his wife.'

'Do you think so?'

Helen wasn't so sure about that, but Sam had other things on his mind. 'You didn't answer my earlier question,' he reminded her. 'Were you happy together?'

'To begin with,' replied Helen honestly. 'Well, Richard seemed happy, anyway. When Melissa was a baby, it was good. It was only as she got older and more—uncontrollable—that she went from being our child to *my* child almost overnight.'

Her father looked distressed. 'Oh, my dear. If only I'd known.' He reached out to squeeze the hand that was lying in her lap. 'Tell me about him. What did he do for a living?'

'Oh, this and that.' Helen didn't want to have

to tell her father that Richard hadn't held down a steady job in all the time she'd known him. That was why she'd had to become the breadwinner, and he'd resented her for it. 'He was working as a courier when he died.'

'A courier?' Sam frowned. 'Not exactly the most suitable job for someone who spent most of his evenings in a pub, I'd have said.'

Helen stared at him. 'How do you—I mean…?'

Sam looked slightly shamefaced now. 'Melissa told me,' he admitted ruefully. 'Oh—believe me, I wasn't questioning her. She just came right out with it.'

'She would,' muttered Helen unhappily. 'I'm sorry if she embarrassed you.'

'She didn't embarrass me.' Her father shook his head. 'But I can easily see that she's quite a handful for you.'

'And the rest.' Helen took another sip of her wine. 'Mmm, this is nice.'

'Don't sound so surprised.' Sam pretended to be offended, but then he frowned again. 'So does Melissa know that Richard wasn't her father?'

'Heavens, no!' Helen was emphatic. 'That was the one thing Richard insisted on. That no one—

including my mother—ever suspected that she wasn't his child.'

'I see.' Sam was thoughtful. Then, getting to his feet, he moved to stand at his office window. 'Did he know who her real father was?'

'No.' Helen's answer was clipped. Then, rather bitterly, she said, 'I notice you don't ask me if *I* know who he was.'

'But, of course, you knew.' Sam swung round then, staring at her with angry eyes. 'Who suggested you didn't?'

Helen shook her head, but her father had connected the dots. 'He did,' he exclaimed harshly. 'Oh, Helen, why didn't you write and tell me?'

A fleeting image of what might have happened if she had briefly crossed her mind. But it had never been an option. She'd believed Milos was married, and flying out to Santoros to confront a married man with his actions would have been quite beyond her. She'd been too young, too scared, and too proud to ask for anyone's help.

CHAPTER FIVE

MILOS drove Melissa back to the vineyard in the late afternoon.

He was still shaken, however, and he gripped the wheel with sweating fingers in a futile attempt to control his emotions. But, God help him, he was staggered by what he'd just discovered.

His original intention had been to spend only a short time at Vassilios. Despite his willingness to entertain the girl, he hadn't really expected Melissa and his sister to hit it off so well.

As he'd anticipated, Rhea had been waiting for him when they had arrived at the villa and, although at eighteen she was scarcely a contemporary of the younger girl, she'd been delighted to meet Melissa.

He acknowledged it was probably because she was so different from the girls Rhea was used to associating with. Girls from wealthy families, like her own, who were generally in awe of their parents. No one could accuse Melissa of that, however, and Rhea, who had always been a bit of a rebel herself, seemed fascinated by her.

From Melissa's point of view, the visit had been a complete success. Rhea had prevailed upon her brother to let the girl stay long enough to have a swim, and, initially, he'd been happy enough to indulge her. After all, he'd had the agenda of an upcoming conference in Athens to study, and it had been quite pleasant hearing the shrieks of girlish laughter coming from the pool.

It wasn't until Rhea had come to find him and ask if Melissa could stay for supper that things had changed. 'We want to practise applying eye make-up,' she said appealingly. 'You know I'm no good at it and Melissa says she is. Her mother probably doesn't stop her from reading women's magazines like Mama does me.'

'Trashy magazines, you mean?' Milos taunted drily. 'Come on, Rhea, Melissa is—what? Twelve? Thirteen years of age at most? I grant you she acts older, but are you seriously telling me—?'

'She's almost fourteen, actually,' Rhea broke in defensively. 'Her birthday's next month, like mine. We're both Geminis.'

Milos's sense of shock was staggering. A sick feeling invaded his stomach, filling his mouth with bile, and a nerve in his temple started to throb. It couldn't be true, he told himself. Rhea must have got it wrong. Melissa couldn't be almost fourteen. If she were...

'Are you all right?'

Rhea noticed his sudden pallor and the knowledge that his sister couldn't be allowed to suspect his thoughts brought a spurious wave of colour back into his cheeks.

'I—yes, I mean—no.' He was at a loss to explain his reaction and it was easier to pretend a momentary giddiness than admit how ill he suddenly felt. 'I'm a little dizzy, that's all.'

'You've been working too hard,' Rhea said at once, evidently relieved it wasn't anything more serious. 'It's so hot today. Perhaps you'll feel better after supper.'

'Perhaps,' Milos agreed, wishing she would just go and leave him alone for a few minutes. 'I'll be all right.'

'So may Melissa stay for supper?' Rhea persisted. 'I'd like her to and it will give you more time to—'

'No!' On that score, Milos knew he had to refuse her. 'I'm sorry, Rhea, but her mother's expecting her back.'

'There are phones,' Rhea said sulkily, and if he hadn't felt so numb he might have wondered if Melissa's influence was already having an effect.

'Another fifteen minutes, that's all,' he said. And, gripping the arms of his chair with a fierceness that bordered on desperation, 'You've already had over an hour.'

'You're no fun, do you know that?' Rhea muttered, apparently already forgetting all about his sudden weakness, and Milos thought that was just as well. 'I don't know what Melissa's going to say.'

But that was the least of his worries. As Rhea flounced out, he was glad she had no idea of the bombshell she'd just delivered. Could what he was thinking possibly be true? he wondered. Surely not. Melissa must have exaggerated her age just as she tended to exaggerate everything else.

Ironically enough, he was desperate to see her then, and as soon as he felt his legs would support him he stumbled across the room to the windows to stare intently at the girl frolicking so happily in his pool.

Melissa had borrowed one of Rhea's swimsuits and he told himself it was the sophistication of the cream and brown bikini that gave her young body such a look of maturity. It had to be, he insisted, but with a hopeless lack of conviction in the thought.

The trouble was, he was then able to see similarities between the two girls, likenesses that until that moment had been distorted, not just by his ignorance, but by Melissa's use of make-up and the ugly clothes she wore.

A black wave of fury swept over him, compounded by his blindness and Helen's total lack of honesty. Why hadn't she told him? She should have told him. If he was Melissa's biological father, he had had a right to know.

But then he remembered something she'd said to him just after she'd stepped off the ferry. She'd asked him about his wife. His wife! How had she known he'd had a wife? He hadn't told her, and he doubted it would have come up in Sam's letters to her. And why was it that whoever had delivered that piece of information hadn't also told her he'd got a divorce? He was baffled.

He sighed now and felt Melissa's eyes slide in his direction. She was sitting beside him in the front of the Mercedes, and now she said curiously, 'Did I do something wrong?'

Immediately, he felt contrite. He hadn't spoken

to her since they'd left Vassilios and he should have guessed she'd be curious.

'Of course not,' he said, glancing her way and experiencing another shock of recognition. Dammit, she had his eyes. And his nose. 'Did you enjoy yourself?'

'I overstayed my welcome, right?' she declared, as if he hadn't spoken. 'Hey, blame your sister, not me.'

'Did I say you'd overstayed your welcome?' he countered shortly, tamping down the impulse to tell her not to speak to him that way. He drew a deep breath. 'I just hope your mother hasn't been worried about you.'

Though she would be, he guessed, suddenly understanding Helen's reluctance to allow him and Melissa to spend time together. She must be living in fear that he'd ask the girl how old she was.

'She's always worrying about me,' said Melissa indifferently, drawing up one foot to rest her heel on the edge of the seat.

Milos hesitated. 'And does she have a reason for that?' he ventured carefully, and Melissa grimaced.

'She thinks so.'

'Why?'

'You don't want to know.'

'I do.' Milos was amazed at how much he wanted to know. 'Doesn't she approve of the way you dress?'

'Did she tell you that?'

'No.'

'So what are you saying? That you don't approve either?'

Milos shook his head. 'We weren't talking about me.'

'No, I know.' She cast him a speculative look. 'So why are you so interested?'

'I'm trying to—to get to know you.'

'Yeah, right.' Melissa was sardonic. 'What you really mean is, you're trying to impress my mum. You didn't really want to take me out. You just wanted to score points with her.'

'You couldn't be more wrong.' In actual fact, Milos couldn't remember why he'd agreed to take her out. It seemed so long ago now. Almost in a parallel universe. He made another effort to get through to her. 'Wouldn't you like us to be—friends?'

'Yeah, yeah.' Patently, she didn't believe him. 'Lucky for you that Rhea was there, wasn't it?'

Lucky? Milos wouldn't have used that word

himself. Yet he acknowledged that sooner or later he was bound to have guessed the truth. Or, at least, he hoped he would.

And there was still Helen…

'So what did she say about me?' Melissa asked suddenly, and once again Milos was nonplussed.

'Who?'

'Rhea, of course. She must have said something. She said she was going to ask you when you were taking me home, but she took ages.'

Milos considered his words very carefully before replying. 'If you must know,' he said, 'she was telling me how much she was enjoying your company. You're very different from the girls she usually mixes with.'

'Tell me about it.' He saw her soft lips compress and for a moment she was incredibly like her mother. 'So I didn't bore her, huh?'

'No.' Milos knew an unexpected surge of compassion, and for the first time he realised he wanted her to like him. 'Were you?'

'Me?' He tried to ignore the way she wedged her foot against the console before continuing. 'Hell, no. It was wicked!'

Wicked?

It wasn't Milos's usual understanding of the

word, but judging from Melissa's expression it meant something good. 'I'm glad,' he said, and he meant it. 'Maybe we can do the same thing again?'

'Maybe.' Melissa regarded him critically. 'So long as you don't start telling me what to do.'

'People do that, do they?'

Melissa shrugged. 'They say I'm uncontrollable.'

'And are you?'

'No.' She was indignant. 'But I can't help it if I find school a drag.'

'Why do you find it a drag?'

Melissa lifted her shoulders again. 'I don't know, do I?'

'I'm sure you do.'

Her jaw jutted. 'You think you're so clever, don't you? You think getting me to talk about school and stuff will make me start to like it?'

'I wouldn't be so presumptuous,' said Milos drily. 'But sometimes if people don't enjoy things, it's because they don't understand what's going on.'

'Are you implying I'm thick?' Melissa huffed. 'You have to be kidding! I can do their assignments standing on my head!'

'So why don't you?'

'Yeah, and be known as a nerd!' Melissa was scornful. 'No, thanks, I prefer to hang with my friends.'

Milos shook his head. 'Are you sure they're not the—what was it you said?—the thick ones? It seems more sensible to me to use your brains if you want to be a success.'

'Hey, did I say I wanted to be a success?' asked Melissa sharply.

'You said you wanted a car like this,' Milos reminded her. 'Cars cost money.'

'What would you know about it?' retorted Melissa rudely. 'I doubt if you've ever had to work for anything in your life.'

Milos expelled a breath. 'That's what you think, is it?'

'Yes. No.' Melissa looked a little shamefaced now. 'I just mean, we're not like you.'

You could be, thought Milos, the realisation that he had a responsibility here striking him with sudden force. But would Helen let him help her? He somehow doubted he would be given the chance.

It didn't surprise him to find Helen perched on the low stone wall that edged the terrace waiting for them. 'Oh, boy, a welcoming committee,' muttered Melissa gloomily. 'Are you gonna tell her what I've said?' She frowned. 'Or were you given orders to sort me out?'

'No one gives me orders,' retorted Milos shortly, and then, meeting Melissa's I-told-you-so look, he pulled a face. 'Not usually, anyway,' he amended, knowing exactly what she was thinking, and they were sharing a smile of mutual understanding when the car halted beside her mother.

Helen was still wearing the skirt and halter she'd had on earlier. The skirt was shorter than she usually wore and Milos's eyes were instantly drawn to her slim arms and long, slender legs. Her hair had come loose from the pony-tail, too, and he wondered if it was because she'd been running anxious hands through it that thick damp strands were clinging sensuously to her flushed cheeks.

She reached for the door as soon as the car had stopped, pulling it open for Melissa to alight. 'I can do it,' Melissa grumbled, and Milos hoped she was sorry because the trip was over. She gave him a rueful look. 'Thanks for the ride.'

'My pleasure,' he said, and, without waiting for her mother to join her, Melissa sauntered up the steps and into the villa. Which left Milos alone with Helen. The ideal opportunity to confront her, he thought. So why did he feel such a reluctance to do so? What if he was wrong?

Her sudden outburst startled him. 'You had no right to be so long,' she exclaimed. 'You must have known I'd be worried about her. What on earth have you been doing?'

Finding out I had a daughter?

But he found he couldn't say that. What if she denied it? What would he do then? Did he really want to find out?

'You knew I was taking her to meet my sister,' he said instead. 'Melissa wanted to have a swim and I didn't think it would be a federal offence.'

Helen wrapped her arms around her waist. 'You should have said so.'

'I thought I just did.'

'No. I mean—oh, it doesn't matter. I expect Melissa enjoyed herself.'

'We all did,' said Milos mildly and saw how her eyes flickered warily to his. 'Rhea, too,' he added, taking pity on her. 'She's not that much older than Melissa.'

'I thought you said she was eighteen?'

'So?'

He dared her to contradict him, but she didn't. 'Well,' she said, with a careless lift of her shoulders, 'Melissa's home now. That's the important thing.'

'Is it?'

She stiffened. 'What else is there?'

Milos gave her a studied look. 'I was wondering if you'd told your father about—us yet.'

'No!' Her denial was vehement, and with his new knowledge he realised how revealing that was.

'Why not?'

'You can ask me that?' Helen's face burned with colour. 'Have you no shame?'

Milos's brows arched. 'Have you?' he countered, stung by her persistence in blaming him for what had happened between them. 'I'd have thought you'd be eager to tell him how I betrayed his trust. But perhaps you have other reasons not to?'

Helen's eyes widened now, giving her the look of a rabbit that had been caught in the headlights of a passing car. 'Wh—what other reasons?' she stammered, evidently caught off guard by his question, and if Milos had had any doubts about Melissa's parentage, her reaction erased them.

'You tell me,' he said, despising himself for feeling sorry for her now. And before she could answer him, Melissa appeared at the top of the steps.

'Hey, Sam says I'm to invite you in for a drink,' she called, addressing herself to Milos, and he could almost feel Helen's relief at the interruption.

But Melissa wasn't finished. Coming down the steps towards them, she took in the evident tension between him and her mother and her eyes narrowed. 'What's going on? Did I interrupt something?'

CHAPTER SIX

HELEN stood in front of the long mirror in her bathroom the following evening regarding her appearance with definite misgivings. Why had she let Melissa persuade her that the black silk top, with its spaghetti straps and plunging neckline—with which, actually, she'd discovered she couldn't wear a bra—was suitable for a family occasion? It looked as if she were wearing her underwear, she fretted. And although the striped black-and-cream skirt that went with it was long, it was also slit almost to her waist.

She groaned. The cheesecloth dress she'd originally chosen would have looked so much more appropriate. But so much more *middle-aged*, as her daughter had said.

And with Melissa behaving uncharacteristically well, Helen had been loath to rock the boat. She didn't know what had happened the day before but evidently Milos's sister had exerted a positive influence over her and, like the black lipstick two days ago, the black nail varnish had also disappeared. Melissa's hair was still streaked with green, of course, but she'd washed the styling wax out of it so that it no longer stuck out in all directions.

Consequently, Helen had felt she was walking on eggshells when Sam had taken them shopping in Aghios Petros this morning. After Milos's attitude when he'd brought her daughter home, she'd wanted nothing to renew the antagonism there had been between her and Melissa before they'd left England. The girl hadn't wanted to come here and sometimes Helen thought she'd been right.

The trouble was, these days it was almost impossible to think about Melissa without associating her with Milos. She hadn't realised the likeness between them would be so pronounced. She suffered agonies of self-doubt when Melissa said how easy he was to talk to, and her reasons for keeping the girl's identity a secret seemed spurious and selfish.

He deserved to know the truth, she thought, and had he been an employee of her father's it would have been so much easier to bear. But he wasn't. He was a wealthy man with unlimited resources; resources he might easily use to convince a judge of her unsuitability as a mother when she'd lied to both her daughter and the man who'd fathered her.

Would a court take into account the fact that she had been only seventeen when Milos had slept with her? He'd seemed so charming, so sincere, that she'd been totally overwhelmed. Her mother hadn't trusted him, but Helen hadn't listened to her. She'd secretly agreed to meet him for a drink and that had sealed her fate.

In fairness to herself, she had to acknowledge that Milos's connection to her father had swung the balance in his favour. She'd been so eager for news of him. In the months since her parents' divorce, she'd regretted not giving Sam a second chance, and she'd been open to any appeal on his behalf.

And if Milos had done what her father had asked him to do and just pleaded his cause, things would have been so different. There'd have been no crazy infatuation on her part, no studied seduction on his.

Instead, Milos's visit had set her relationship with her father back a dozen years or more. Once her daughter had been born, there'd been no going back. She'd been married to Richard Shaw and her future had been set.

She shivered now, swallowing the unwilling anticipation she was feeling at the knowledge that soon she'd be seeing Milos again. The day before, he'd only stayed long enough to offer Sam his apologies, making the excuse that he had work to do at home. But this evening there was to be a buffet dinner in honour of herself and Melissa, and naturally Maya had prevailed upon him to join them.

All day, the delicious smells of cooking food had pervaded the villa. Not that Maya was doing the actual cooking herself. Sam had confided that several women from the nearby village had come to supplement their small staff, and Helen's offer to help had been politely—but conspicuously—declined.

Which was how she and Melissa had been able to go shopping with Sam that morning. It had given them both the chance to supplement their meagre wardrobes—Helen had brought little from home, believing her father to be dying—and even Melissa had shown an unaccustomed interest in buying clothes.

Now, as Helen leant towards the mirror to apply a bronze glaze to her eyelids Melissa appeared in the bathroom doorway behind her. Helen saw the girl's reflection before she saw the girl herself and it gave her time to school her expression before Melissa noticed.

She didn't want to appear too enthusiastic about her daughter's appearance. That had always been the way to turn her off. But it was hard to be offhand when Melissa looked so attractive. The sleeveless cotton dress was perfect, and lime green was definitely her colour.

To her relief, the girl's attention was immediately caught by what Helen was wearing and a triumphant expression appeared on her face. 'Do I know how to choose gear or do I know how to choose gear?' she crowed delightedly. 'God, Mum, you look really hot! And at least ten years younger than you would have done in that sack you'd chosen for yourself.'

Helen glanced down at herself. 'You don't think this outfit is too—young for me?' she asked uncertainly, and Melissa snorted.

'Stop stressing, Mum,' she said. 'You look great. Milos is going to be well impressed.'

Helen caught her breath. 'I'm not trying to impress anybody,' she protested. 'Least of all Milos Stephanides.' She hesitated. 'I just don't want to look like a—a—' the word 'tart' hovered on her tongue, but she couldn't say that without offending her daughter '—like a teenager.'

'With your boobs? You wish.' Melissa grimaced. 'Come on. I'm wearing what you wanted, the least you can do is do the same.'

Which said everything, thought Helen, resigning herself to her fate. And Melissa did look nice, if older than her mother could have wished. As they went down the stone staircase Helen couldn't help wondering if it wouldn't have been safer for both of them if Melissa had maintained her 'goth' image.

It was almost dark when they stepped outside, following the buzz of voices from the terrace. A velvet dusk had fallen and strings of coloured bulbs suspended from the trees gave the scene a magical illumination.

Already a small crowd of people were gathered, laughing and talking and exchanging gossip that Helen couldn't hope to understand. It was obvious they all knew one another and they didn't need the drinks her father was generously dispensing to loosen their tongues.

She saw Maya first, looking happy for once, with Sam on one side of her and Alex on the other. But Helen's eyes were instantly drawn to the tall man standing right beside them, his dark features rendered positively sinister in the shadowy light.

But she wasn't allowed to carry this thought to its logical conclusion. Her father had seen them and he came eagerly towards them, his gaunt face alight with obvious approval.

'You look—you *both* look splendid,' he said, catching one of their hands in each of his, and Helen noticed that Melissa didn't bridle at his enthusiasm. 'You don't know how proud I am to have you here with me at last.'

'Mum looks good, doesn't she?' Melissa asked slyly, indifferent to their audience. 'I chose this outfit. Do you like it?'

Helen wanted to shrink into the woodwork, but Sam wasn't at all perturbed. 'I do,' he said. 'You've got taste, little one. But, you know, your mother's a beautiful woman.'

Helen blushed at this, and before Melissa could say anything else to embarrass her Sam drew them both forward. 'Come,' he said. 'These people are all dying to meet you. Let me introduce you.'

To Helen's relief, most of the guests spoke at least a smattering of English and, as Sam had said, they were all eager to meet her. Sam had evidently told them that she was a widow and she was offered frequent condolences for her sad loss.

Milos's sister was there and, after meeting Rhea, Helen could understand why Melissa liked her so much. It might also explain why her daughter was on her best behaviour, but Helen was too relieved to look too hard for explanations.

Alex was a familiar face, and after Sam returned to the bar he seemed to appoint himself her protector. 'You will have realised by now that we Greeks are always happy to have an excuse for a party,' he said drily. 'But I'm so happy for Sam. I know how much he's missed you all these years.'

'I've missed him, too,' murmured Helen, only now realising how much she had done so. Then, with a frown, 'You must have been very young when your mother and—and my father got together.'

'I was ten,' agreed Alex with a nod. 'Although I call your father Sam, he's always been like a father to me.'

'I'm sure.'

Helen wanted to ask more and, as if sensing her curiosity, Alex continued, 'My own father was a fisherman. He was drowned before I was born.'

He paused. 'He never knew about me. He and my mother were not married, you see.'

Helen nodded, sympathising as much with Maya as with him. It must have been hard for her, too, with a baby on the way and no husband. She knew the feeling.

It was perhaps unfortunate that Milos should choose that moment to join them. Helen visibly jumped when he spoke to her, and she knew Alex had noticed.

'*Kalispera*, Helen,' Milos greeted her smoothly, and if he'd noticed her alarm he didn't mention it. 'You're looking well this evening.'

'Thank you. I'm fine.' She spoke a little stiffly, but she couldn't help it. Then, because something more was expected of her, she added, 'It was good of you to join us.'

Milos's lips thinned. 'It was my pleasure,' he said, the innocent words belied by his grave expression. He looked down at the half-empty glass of retsina in her hand. 'Alex, your stepsister is in need of a refill. Can you do that for her?'

'Oh, but I—'

Helen was about to say she didn't want another drink, but Milos had already whipped the glass out of her hand and handed it to the other man.

Alex looked a little doubtful, but he was too polite to argue with a guest.

'*Kanena provlima,*' he said, good-naturedly, and
with a brief word to excuse himself he walked
away.

'He said, no problem,' Milos offered artlessly,
as soon as they were alone, and Helen gave him
an accusing look.

'I didn't want another drink,' she said tersely.
'Please don't presume to make my decisions for
me.'

'Did I do that?' Milos lifted his glass to his lips
before continuing and she was unwillingly treated
to the sight of the muscles moving sinuously in his
throat. 'I thought it might help you to relax,' he
went on, lowering his glass again. 'You're strung
as tight as a mandolin.'

'And whose fault is that?'

Milos's dark brows ascended. 'I assume you're
making me the culprit.'

'Who else?'

'Why?' His eyes rested briefly on her mouth
and she felt the heat of that sensuous appraisal
liquefying her insides. 'I admit, I'm flattered, but
as we know one another so well—'

'We don't know one another *so well*,' she retorted hotly. 'We—we hardly know one another at all.'

'Oh, I think we do.' Milos held her gaze now, and she was helplessly aware of how easily he could turn the tables on her. There was a pregnant silence and then he said, 'Your daughter likes me.'

Helen felt suddenly chilled in spite of the warm evening. 'And that's supposed to be a recommendation?' she demanded at last, albeit a little faintly. 'Melissa befriends the most unsuitable people.'

'Yes, so she was telling me.'

Helen's jaw dropped. 'She told you?'

'Mmm.' He was infuriatingly casual. 'We had quite a conversation on the way back from Vassilios.'

Helen had known that, of course. Had seen the conspiratorial smile that had passed between them before her daughter had got out of his car. She'd tried to put it to the back of her mind, had convinced herself it meant nothing. Melissa hadn't mentioned it and Helen had been too proud to question her.

But now she gazed at Milos with worried eyes. What had Melissa told him to put that look of smug complacency on his face? Not the truth,

obviously. But something he considered powerful enough to taunt her in this way.

'How long has she been dodging school?' he
asked abruptly, and Helen gulped.

'How do you—?' Helen broke off and rephrased
the question. 'Did Melissa tell you that?'

'She didn't have to,' said Milos flatly. 'It goes
with the territory. She hangs about with losers.
What else can she do?'

Helen wet her dry lips. 'They're not all losers,'
she began, and then halted again when Milos gave
her a knowing look. 'Well, all right. We have had
some trouble with—with truancy,' she admitted.
'But all teen—all *children*,' she corrected herself
hurriedly, 'go through a rebellious period.'

'And that's all you think it is? A rebellious period.'

'What else could it be?' Helen was defensive.

'It could be the start of a lifetime of under-
achieving,' said Milos brutally. 'What the hell
kind of example did your late husband set for her?
The girl doesn't even think education is worth
the effort.'

Helen bent her head. 'I didn't ask for your
opinion.'

'You did, actually.' He was relentless. 'In any case, you're getting it for free.'

'You mean, you can't resist interfering in my life.' Helen glanced uneasily about her. 'Where's Alex? I hope he didn't take your intrusion as a reason to stay away.'

Milos shrugged. 'He'll be back.'

'And until then, you're going to annoy me.' Helen gave a sigh. 'Isn't there some other woman desperate for your attention? Why pick on me?'

Milos gave a short, mirthless laugh. 'Perhaps you're good for my ego.'

Helen shook her head. 'What do you really want, Milos? I can't believe you're enjoying this any more than I am.'

'You're wrong.' Milos leant towards her, his wine-scented breath enveloping her, causing a film of heat to spread unchecked all across her body. 'We need to talk, Helen. Don't you agree?'

Helen's legs felt like jelly. 'We're talk-ing now.'

'Not like this.' Milos's eyes bored into hers. 'We have things to say to one another that are best said in private.'

'Wh—what things?'

Milos's hand came up to stroke the exposed skin of her shoulder. 'Oh, I'm sure we'll think of something,' he murmured softly. 'Like why you tremble when I touch you.' His fingers trailed down her arm, pausing to caress the curve of her breast. 'Or why you're not yelling your head off because I'm taking liberties no decent woman would permit.'

'Or no decent man would perpetrate,' she got out tremulously. 'Leave me alone, Milos. Please!'

'I can't do that,' he said huskily, and she felt the brush of his mouth against her temple.

She was sure he was going to kiss her mouth and she was ashamed to admit that she tilted her head back almost compulsively. But then, abruptly, he stepped away from her, and as her brain clicked back into gear she saw Melissa and his sister standing at the other side of the terrace, watching them.

So, no belated twinge of conscience, she thought bitterly. With her history, she should have known better.

It was perhaps predictable that Alex should choose that moment to return with her drink. 'There you are,' he said, handing the refilled glass to her, and, uncaring what she'd told Milos, Helen gulped at it greedily.

'Thanks,' she said, when she lowered the glass, aware that both men were regarding her with differing expressions. 'I needed that.' And let Milos make what he liked of it!

In the event, her defiance was wasted. As if suddenly losing interest in her, Milos paused only long enough to say *'Signomi,'* which she knew meant 'Excuse me,' before leaving them. He strode away towards the buffet tables where Maya was more than happy to welcome him.

'Milos seems annoyed,' said Alex, watching the other man with thoughtful eyes. 'Has he said anything to upset you?'

'To upset me?' Helen's voice rose on the automatic denial. She struggled to steady herself. 'Um—no. We—er—we were just talking about old times, that's all.'

She realised too late that that had probably not been the most sensible thing to say when Alex frowned. 'I didn't know you and Milos were old friends,' he remarked quietly. 'How did you meet?'

'Oh—it was years ago,' said Helen hastily. 'Milos was on holiday in England and my father asked him to—to look me up.'

'Really?' Alex was obviously intrigued. 'You know, I've never known Milos go to England except on business.'

That'd be right, thought Helen cynically. She'd

been just another piece of business. A piece of something, anyway, and she'd been the one to pay the price.

CHAPTER SEVEN

IT WAS still early when Milos stepped out onto the balcony of his bedroom at Vassilios.

Although the rising sun was already spreading fingers of gold over the grey-blue ocean, a cool breeze drifted about his bare legs and chilled the sweat drying between his shoulder blades. Silk boxers hung dangerously low on his hips, but he didn't notice. A sense of dissatisfaction was overriding his awareness of everything, including the beauty of the morning.

He'd slept badly again and frustration was making him not only weary, but short-tempered. Dammit, he ought to have had what was troubling him out with Helen the night before and it infuriated him that once again he'd let her off the hook.

But a combination of his aggressiveness and her fragility had once again defeated him. Besides, he hadn't been able to keep his hands off her and that had definitely not helped his cause.

Yet this was an emotional business, an emotional time bomb even, and he knew he was a fool for letting her run rings around him. Why did he feel this foolish need to protect her, even from himself? Why, when she looked at him with those wide haunted eyes, did he begin to doubt his own beliefs?

Whatever, the party the Campbells had arranged for them hadn't been a suitable place to conduct a serious conversation, and Milos had left as soon as he decently could. Rhea had objected. She'd wanted to stay for the dancing, which was to follow the buffet. But Milos had told her rather baldly that, unless she wanted to find her own way home, she would have to leave with him.

The whole evening had been a disaster, he acknowledged, watching the birds scavenging for food on the beach below his balcony. And what was really bugging him was the fact that he was leaving for Athens later today. The conference on world ecology, which he was forced to attend, began the next day, and it would be at least three more days before he could get back to the island.

Frustration swept over him again. He had to talk to Helen before he left. He had to get her to admit the truth about Melissa. Until she did, he was just whistling in the wind.

* * *

Even Sam was surprised when Helen was called to the phone and returned to say that Rhea Stephanides had invited her and Melissa to lunch.

'I don't know why she's invited me,' she murmured, despite Melissa's sudden enthusiasm. 'I hardly know the girl.'

'I do,' said her daughter eagerly. She frowned at her mother. 'You didn't refuse, did you?'

'No-o.'

Helen admitted that she hadn't, even though she was still doubtful, and Melissa was pleased. 'I can always go on my own,' she said consideringly. 'I don't need you to baby me.' She turned to her grandfather. 'You'll take me, won't you, Sam?'

Helen hesitated. 'Melissa—'

'I think you should both go,' Sam declared firmly, and for once Maya agreed with him.

'It's not as if Milos will be there,' she said smugly. 'From what I can gather, he's leaving for Athens this morning.'

'The conference. Of course.' Her husband endorsed this statement. 'It's a gathering of oil producers discussing the ways of reducing pollution on world ecology,' he explained to Helen. 'Milos is one of the keynote speakers.'

'I see.'

Helen was just absorbing this when Melissa spoke up again. 'There you go, Mum,' she said. 'You don't have to worry. This isn't some sneaky way for Milos to get you on your own.'

Helen's face blazed with colour. 'I never thought it was,' she protested hotly, conscious that both Maya and her father were aware of her embarrassment. 'I wish you wouldn't say things like that, Melissa. I—I hardly know the man.'

'He'd like to know you, though,' said Melissa slyly. 'Rhea and me saw you together last night, remember?'

'You saw us talking, that's all,' exclaimed Helen, giving her father a humiliated look. 'Honestly, she has such a vivid imagination!'

'Don't let her upset you,' said Sam mildly, his eyes twinkling at his granddaughter. 'She's only teasing you. We all know Milos is easy on the eye, but I don't imagine you're foolish enough to take him seriously. You've got the wrong idea, Melissa. I think you should apologise.'

Melissa looked sulky now and Helen's heart sank at the prospect of what she was sure was to come. But in the event all Melissa said was, 'But Mum does like Milos; I know she does. And he couldn't take his eyes off her when we were having supper.'

Sam sighed, but it was Maya who chose to answer the girl. 'You're imagining things. It's like your grandfather says, Milos has always been popular with the opposite sex. But you shouldn't run away with the idea that he might be interested in an Englishwoman. Greeks marry Greeks. It's the way it should be.'

'You didn't—' began Melissa, but before she could dig a bigger hole for herself Sam spoke again.

'Be that as it may, I do agree that Maya might have a point. I think Milos has had enough of marriage. I don't think he's likely to burn his hands again.'

An hour later, Helen found herself in the front seat of her father's Jeep. He'd offered to drive them to the Stephanides's villa at San Rocco himself after Melissa had taken her mother's breath away by apologising for upsetting them all.

'We're almost there,' Sam said suddenly, pointing to the white walls of a villa just visible above some trees. 'That's Aristotle's place up there. It doesn't have a pool,' he added for Melissa's benefit, 'but the views are magnificent.'

'You've been here, then?'

Melissa loosened her seat belt and leaned forward to rest her arms along the backs of their seats, and her grandfather nodded. 'Many times,' he agreed. 'As you know, the Stephanideses are distantly related to Maya.'

'And she doesn't let us forget it,' remarked Melissa unthinkingly, before adding, 'Sorry. It looks great.'

'It is.' Her grandfather wasn't offended. 'It's not as modern as Milos's place, of course, but I think you'll like it.'

Rhea came out to meet them as the Jeep reached the gravelled forecourt. She was wearing an ankle-length wrap-around skirt and a sleeveless shirt, tied at her midriff, and Helen saw the way Melissa checked out her appearance as she got out of the vehicle.

The two girls greeted one another warmly, but although Rhea invited Sam in he said he'd be on his way. Rhea also offered to see that Helen and Melissa arrived home safely and Helen guessed her father would be glad not to have to make the journey a second time.

She was also relieved to see that Rhea looked more her age this morning. Last evening, the resemblance between the two girls had seemed obvious. But today Rhea looked older, more mature. Which was reassuring.

'You both look nice,' she remarked now, surveying her guests as they entered the deliciously cool entrance hall of the villa. She gestured towards Melissa's low-rise cotton trousers. 'Are they new?'

'Yes.' Melissa preened at the unaccustomed praise. 'And Mum's dress is new, too. Do you like it?'

'Very much,' said Rhea politely, but Helen guessed the cheap sundress, in shades of blue and green, was not something Rhea herself would ever dream of wearing.

'It was kind of you to invite us,' she said, hoping to change the subject. 'Melissa enjoyed herself so much at Vassilios the other day.'

'Y-e-s.' Rhea drew out the word as if she wasn't exactly sure she meant it. 'But I'm afraid I'm not the person you should thank for the invitation.'

'I'm sorry…'

Helen was struggling to comprehend what she meant when a dark shadow emerged through the archway to their right. 'No,' said Milos pleasantly, smiling at Melissa who had turned to give her mother a triumphant grin. And, as Helen's eyes adjusted to the light he added, 'I fear I'm to blame. Will you forgive me?'

For a moment, Helen couldn't say anything. But then, her eyes turning from Milos's dark face to Rhea's and back again, she said, 'I thought—that is—Maya said you were leaving for Athens today.'

'I am.' Milos was clearly visible now, a tall, disturbing figure in a black shirt and matching jeans. He glanced at his sister. 'Why don't you ask Marisa to bring us some refreshments, Rhea? We'll be on the terrace.'

'I'll go with you, Rhea,' said Melissa at once, and, although Helen wanted to stop her, she knew she could speak more freely without her daughter's watching gaze.

'Is that all right with you, Milos?'

Rhea looked to her brother for his approval and Helen's nails dug into her palms. They were all in thrall to this arrogant man, she thought helplessly. Oh, God, why had she ever agreed to come?

'The terrace is this way,' declared Milos politely when they were alone, and, although Helen wanted to tell him to go to hell, she obediently followed him along a cool tiled hallway whose thick walls guarded against the heat. 'My grandfather built this place more than sixty years ago,' he volunteered as they walked. 'There was no road in those days and it was a convenient hide-out for members of the resistance forces during the last war.'

'How interesting.'

Helen made no attempt to hide her sarcasm, but even she couldn't deny a gasp of surprise when they emerged onto the terrace. She hadn't re-alised the Jeep had climbed so high, but the hill-side tumbling away to whitewashed villages, with the spires of hidden churches peeping through the mass of greenery, was breathtaking.

'impressive, *ne*?' murmured Milos, resting his back against the stone wall that ringed the terrace at waist height. 'It was originally built as a—what would you say?—a holiday home. Athens, in the heat of summer, is not to be recommended.'

'How lucky to have the choice,' remarked Helen drily, resting her hands on the top of the wall some distance from him. 'So where are your parents now?'

'They're cruising in the Pacific,' said Milos, with some reluctance. 'And before you make some other scathing comment, I should tell you that my father had a heart attack at the beginning of the year and has been forced to retire. Other-

wise, he would be attending the Athens conference himself.'

Helen knew a momentary feeling of guilt but
she refused to let him see it. 'I'm sorry,' she said
tersely, and she was. She wouldn't wish ill health
on anyone.

There was silence between them for a few seconds. Then Milos turned and put his hand on the
wall only inches from hers. She tensed automatically, but all he did was abrade the stone with his
thumb. So why did she feel as if it were her skin
he was stroking?

'Would you like to see where I live when I'm
staying on the island?' he asked suddenly, his
voice huskier than before, and Helen had to steel
herself not to move away from him.

'Why would I want to see your house?' she
asked shortly. 'Melissa's told me all about it.'

'Word of mouth is not the same as actually seeing it for yourself,' he insisted softly. His eyes lingered on her mouth before moving down to the
low vee of her cleavage. 'Come with me, Helen.
I want to prove to you I'm not the selfish bastard
you think I am.'

'I don't have any thoughts about you, good or
otherwise,' she countered hurriedly, keeping her

voice steady with an effort. She glanced behind her. 'Melissa and your sister are taking an awfully long time. Do you think I should go and hurry them up?'

'I think you should stay exactly where you are,' retorted Milos harshly. His hand suddenly moved to close about her wrist and she wondered if he could feel her pulse racing against his palm. 'How long are you going to keep this up, Helen?' His eyes glittered dangerously. 'How long are you going to deny that you wanted me as much as I wanted you all those years ago?'

'Wanted being the operative word,' said Helen, her breath coming in short, painful gasps. 'You forget, I didn't know you were married, Milos. I soon changed my mind about you when your wife explained why you'd really come to England.'

'My wife explained?' Milos looked baffled now, but that didn't stop him from using his hold on her wrist to jerk her closer. 'My wife and I were separated long before I came to England. I don't know where you've got your information from, but I can assure you that's the truth.'

'A pity your wife didn't see it that way,' Helen countered, uncomfortably aware of how close he was. 'Let me go, Milos. Or do you want your sister to see how badly you treat your guests?'

'Badly?' Milos was scathing. 'You don't know how badly I want to treat you. And I don't particularly care what Rhea thinks.' His hot gaze was almost suffocating her now and she was unhappily aware that her body wasn't responding as it should. He had only to touch her and she trembled. No matter how detached she tried to be, it seemed to have a will of its own. 'I wonder how you'd react if you were naked,' he added thickly. 'Would that have any effect on your treacherous little soul?'

Helen swallowed, unable to prevent herself from looking up at him. 'Would it have any effect on yours?' she countered, not knowing where the provocative words came from, but unable to take them back.

'Oh, yes.' His response was immediate, and now he turned, imprisoning her against the wall behind her. His taut body pressed hers into the stones, letting her feel every bone and angle. 'Now tell me that what we had meant nothing to you,' he exhorted roughly. 'Tell me you have no lasting memories of that night.'

Even as his tongue trailed a wet path along her

jawline panic gripped her. What did he mean? What was he saying? Was all of this—this planned seduction designed to get her to confess?

Dear God, if it was true, he was clever. Because right then she was tempted—unbearably tempted—to give in. With one of his thighs wedged between her legs and her breasts crushed against his chest, it would be so easy to delude herself into thinking this meant something.

Thankfully, it didn't happen. His mouth had barely brushed her lips when they heard the sound of voices heading in their direction. Melissa and Rhea were laughing and talking together as they came to find them and, despite what he'd said earlier, it was enough to cause Milos to utter a muffled oath and put a decent distance between them before the two girls appeared.

Helen didn't recover so easily. Although the kiss had been brief, her face was flooded with colour and she was sure Melissa would notice. Her daughter always noticed everything.

But if she did, she said nothing, and it was left to Rhea to say with some concern, 'Is it too hot for you out here, Helen?'

'Um—no, I'm fine,' murmured Helen quickly, but Rhea still looked doubtful.

'We can sit in the shade,' she said, nodding to where a trellis overhung with bougainvillea sheltered a wicker table and chairs. 'Marisa is on her way with the tray.'

'How nice.'

Helen was sure she must sound as out of it as she was feeling and she was glad when Melissa exclaimed, 'Rhea and me are going down to the beach for a swim, Mum. You can come with us, if you like.'

'That sounds inviting.' Helen didn't even have the will to correct her grammar, but then Milos intervened.

'I'm planning on showing your mother a little of the island this morning,' he inserted smoothly, and Helen was amazed at his arrogance. 'I believe she's seen very little of it so far.'

'Oh, I think a swim sounds much more appealing than riding around in a hot car,' Helen protested, not looking at him as she spoke. He thought he could just order her around and, remembering what he'd been doing before the two girls had arrived, she rather thought he was right.

'You can swim at Vassilios,' he declared, evidently determined to have his own way. 'I'm sure Rhea and Melissa don't need a chaperon, do you?'

Melissa quickly came to the same conclusion. 'Yeah, that's right, Mum,' she said as Marisa appeared with the tray. And, obviously hoping to end the discussion, 'Mmm, lemonade! I love that stuff.'

'So—it's agreed.' Milos seated himself opposite Helen as Rhea took charge of the coffee-pot. 'We'll meet back here for lunch, *ne*?'

No one else was willing to argue with him, but after the girls had driven away in Rhea's open-topped buggy Helen faced him angrily.

'I'm not going with you, Milos,' she said, aware that at least Marisa was within calling distance if she needed her. 'If you insist on talking, we can. But we'll do it here. Not at Vassilios.'

Milos regarded her from between lowered lids. 'Are you afraid of me, Helen?'

Hell, yes, she thought. She was afraid of him. But she wasn't going to tell him that. 'I just think it would be more—sensible if we stayed here,' she insisted. 'Melissa and Rhea won't be long.'

'Long enough,' said Milos, crossing his arms over his body. 'Come on. What have you got to lose?'

CHAPTER EIGHT

BEFORE he'd met Helen again, Milos had sworn to himself that he'd never let another woman get under his skin. All those years ago, when he'd let his senses get the better of his reason, he'd bitterly regretted it. He'd promised himself he'd never do anything like that again, and, although he hadn't been a monk all these years, no woman had ever come close to achieving what Helen had achieved, almost without her being aware of it.

To begin with, he hadn't wanted to believe he was never going to see her again. Even when she'd run out on him, he'd tried to find excuses for her, and it was only when she'd refused to speak to him that he'd had to accept that as far as she was concerned it was over.

He'd suffered agonies of remorse in the months after his return to Greece, not just because of his own feelings of betrayal, but because he'd let Sam down as well. It had taken years for him to regain his own self-respect and now he was in danger of losing it all over again.

He was such a fool! He'd barely brushed her mouth with his lips and he'd wanted to strip her clothes from her and bury himself in her hot little body. When Melissa and Rhea had interrupted them, he'd wanted to howl in frustration. Yet how could he feel anything but contempt for a woman who persisted in lying to him over and over again?

Now, with her sitting beside him in the front seat of his father's elderly Aston Martin, he acknowledged that whatever happened he was never going to be indifferent to her. But he would deal with it, he told himself. He couldn't let her ruin his life a second time.

He'd borrowed his father's car because he'd ridden to San Rocco on the back of his Harley. He'd needed the unleashed power of the motorbike to clear his brain of the cobwebs that had clouded it when he'd woken up. Besides, he hadn't known how he'd react having her spread thighs pressed against his butt. There was only so much a man could take.

Even so, there was no denying that being with her, feeling the heat of her warm body only inches from his, fired his blood. He was so stimulated, he could smell her—smell the flowery perfume he'd noticed once before, detect the tantalising scent of an arousal she'd already denied.

Taking her to Vassilios might be a mistake, too, he reflected. Did he really want to remember her there, at the heart of his existence? It was all right to tell himself that, at Vassilios, he was his own master. Only he realised how specious that description was.

The villa lay at the edge of a deep valley, where scarlet poppies and pink and white campion dotted the lush pastures where his horses grazed. The villa itself sprawled across a wide plateau, with white-railed paddocks surrounding it and a stream meandering under a stone bridge and down to a sandy shoreline.

Milos heard Helen catch her breath when she saw his home and was foolishly pleased by her reaction. He'd wanted her to like the place, particularly as she'd been so reluctant to come here. Besides, he was proud of it. The house had been built to his own design.

Stelios appeared from around the back of the building as they drove up to the house. The old man and his wife, Andrea, looked after the place for him. In recent years, Stelios had become troubled with arthritis, and Milos had had to employ a couple of younger men to do the rough work. But the old man was very proud of his position and he never let any of the younger employees forget he was the boss.

Now, his beady eyes fastened on Helen as they drew up, and Milos guessed he was already speculating about their relationship. After all, he seldom brought any women to Vassilios.

'Ya, Stelios,' Milos greeted him now, pushing open his door and getting out of the car. Then, in his own language, 'Would you ask Andrea to bring us some refreshments? We'll be on the veranda.'

'Sigoora, kirieh.' Certainly, sir.

Stelios spoke only a little English, and although Milos guessed the old man expected him to introduce his guest, he didn't. Right now, he had more important things on his mind.

Milos nodded his thanks and then, seeing that Helen had already alighted from the car, he spread one hand to indicate she should precede him up the shallow steps and into the house.

They entered a large atrium that rose through two floors to a circular glazed ceiling above. The staircase giving access to the upper floor fanned

out from its centre, while open pocket doors on either side of the foyer revealed elegantly furnished
living and dining areas.

Milos saw at once that Helen was impressed by
her surroundings. The feeling of light and space
he'd incorporated into his drawings, and which
the architect had followed so meticulously, gave
the area a cool airiness that owed nothing to artificial means.

Bypassing the living and dining areas, Milos led
the way along a screened hallway, and out onto the
veranda at the back of the villa. Here, cushioned
chairs were set in the shade of the overhanging
balcony, the magnificent view of the ocean beyond an ever-changing backdrop.

He heard Helen draw in a breath when she saw
the mosaic-tiled pool that lay below the patio.
Curved stone steps led down, either into the pool
itself or onto the stone apron that surrounded it.
Canopied lounge chairs looked colourful and
inviting in the sunlight, and she wouldn't have
been human if she hadn't seen some beauty in
the scene.

'Shall we sit?' suggested Milos, indicating the
chairs in the shade of the veranda, but Helen
moved towards the steps leading down to the pool.

Standing with her back to him, she was unaware of how the sunlight limned the rounded curve of her hips and her long legs, even through her dress. But Milos was aware of everything about her, and he pushed his hands into his jeans' pockets, wondering if she had any idea how tense he was.

'You have a lovely view,' she said, glancing back over her shoulder as the errant breeze caught a strand of her hair and blew it across her mouth.

Didn't he just? thought Milos, but he didn't say anything. After all, he could hardly tell her what was in his thoughts.

She lifted her hand then to tuck the silky coil behind her ear, the thin fabric of her dress now drawn taut against her breasts. Did she know how provocative it was to lick her lips like that? he wondered. Or was this just a studied attempt to distract him?

'So,' she said as he fought the urge to go and make her as aware of him as he was of her, 'what are we really doing here?'

Milos pulled his hands out of his pockets and thrust them through his hair. 'I'm sure you know,' he said, pleased that he sounded almost reasonable. 'Why don't you sit with me and we'll talk?'

'You talk, Milos. You're the one with all the

questions,' she retorted swiftly. 'Tell me what you're thinking and I'll try and answer you.'

But it wasn't that easy. Nothing ever was, he acknowledged grimly. His image of her now kept being overlaid with his image of how she'd looked the first time he'd seen her. A tall, slender girl, in the uniform jeans and sweatshirt she'd worn to the sixth-form college she'd been attending, she'd taken his breath away. He remembered his reaction to her then as if it had all happened yesterday and not more than fourteen years ago...

Milos was having afternoon tea in the sitting room with Sheila Campbell when Helen breezed into the house.

'Hey, who does that swish car belong to?' she was beginning—meaning the powerful Saab he had hired for the duration of his stay—as she came into the room. Then she came to an abrupt halt when she saw their visitor rising politely from the sofa at her entrance.

It was hard to say who was the most embarrassed at that moment. Sheila—who had admitted him to the house with obvious reluctance once she'd heard of his association with her ex-husband; Helen—because of the brashness of her arrival;

or Milos himself—who knew he was here under false pretences and who had never expected Sam Campbell's daughter would look anything like this.

Because Helen was beautiful, with the kind of untouched English beauty poets wrote about in books. Violet eyes, a faultless complexion, a mouth a man could only think of possessing. In other words, she was gorgeous, the tight faded jeans and navy sweat shirt in no way detracting from her appeal.

Her hair was fairly long, a thick blonde mane that had been streaked even by the weaker English sun. She wore it drawn back in a loose coil at her nape, and Milos guessed it would feel as lush and silky as it looked.

He was staring, he knew, but he couldn't help it. From the moment her eyes had met his, he'd been aware of the connection between them. He wanted to get to know her; no, he *needed* to get to know her. It was a long time, if ever, since he'd felt such an instantaneous attraction before.

Her mother spoiled it, of course.

'This is Mr Stephanides,' she said stiffly. 'He works with your father. He's on holiday at the moment and apparently your father asked him to look us up.'

Milos saw the way Helen's face froze at the mention of her father. It was as if whatever emotion his name inspired was not for public consumption. 'My father?' she said stiffly. 'You know my father?' And when Milos inclined his head, she murmured reluctantly, 'Is he all right?'

'He's fine,' Milos assured her, silently acknowledging what Sam had already told him: that Helen had taken her mother's side during the divorce. 'But he sends you his love, naturally. I believe it's over a year since you've seen him.'

'Almost two,' Sheila Campbell broke in irritably, not liking being left out. 'Not that that means anything to him. Helen knows what her father thinks of her. He made that very clear when he left us for that Greek woman. If you've come to plead his cause, Mr Stephanides, you're wasting your time.'

'I haven't—that is—' Milos knew he mustn't show his hand too soon. Sam had warned him that Sheila would try to block any communication between him and Helen. By taking Sam's side, he was only going to alienate them both. 'As I say,

I'm on holiday at the moment. As I know—few people in England, Sam gave me your address.'

'He had no right to,' said Sheila Campbell at once. 'I know what his game is. He wants you to go back and tell him that we're only struggling along without him. What's the matter? Isn't his second marriage working either? Well, he needn't think he can come back here. We're managing very nicely without him, aren't we, Helen?'

'Oh—I—sure.'

Helen looked a little discomforted by her mother's animosity, but it might be only wishful thinking on his part. 'Sam's fine,' he said anyway. And happy, he could have added, feeling the need to defend the other man. But he held his tongue and turned to Helen. 'That's my car out there, actually. I'm glad you think it's—what was it you said? Swish?' He smiled, trying to reach her despite her mother's presence. 'It's not mine, I'm afraid. I've just hired it from a rental agency.'

Helen gave a careless shrug. 'I didn't recognise it, that's all.'

'Helen's not interested in expensive cars,' Sheila Campbell broke in crisply. Then, looking at her daughter, 'I expect you've got homework to do, Helen. Don't let us keep you. Helen's at sixth-form college, Mr Stephanides. She's hoping to go to university.'

Helen was evidently glad to escape. With a brief word of farewell, she left the room as quickly as she'd entered it. Milos wanted to detain her. He wanted to tell her he'd come to see her, not her mother, but that was impossible at the moment. Apart from anything else, if Sheila Campbell even suspected his motives, she'd probably forbid her daughter from having anything to do with him, and he had no real confidence in his own ability to make Helen listen to what he had to say.

It was two days before he saw her again.

Deciding the Saab was too noticeable, Milos had changed it for a more popular model, realising that if he wanted to get in touch with Helen he would have to do so surreptitiously. Consequently, he'd parked some distance from the house the following morning, hoping he might be able to intercept his quarry on her way to college.

He'd been too late. Although he'd wasted the better part of the morning waiting for her, the only person he'd seen was Mrs Campbell evidently on her way to work. She'd backed an ancient Ford out of the driveway and taken off in the opposite direction, leaving Milos not really knowing if Helen had already left or not.

He'd considered waiting for her after school, but that had presented too many problems. For one thing, he didn't know where the school was or from what direction she'd approach the house, and for another, her mother would expect her to be home at a certain time. Any deviation from her usual schedule might make her mother suspicious.

Milos took up his position the following morning much earlier than the day before. Hunched over a takeaway coffee, he thought how ludicrous it was that he had to act this way. He hadn't had time to shave, and he'd had no breakfast. Not exactly the scenario he'd anticipated when he'd agreed to Sam's request to speak to his daughter.

Once again, the first person to appear was Sheila Campbell. As on the previous morning, she reversed out of her gateway and took off down the street. Milos scowled. Dammit, if Helen was going to school, wouldn't her mother have given her a lift? He couldn't have missed her again. It was barely eight o'clock.

He waited until after nine before making any move. When he'd attended university in England, schools had started well before a quarter past nine.

She'd either left already without his seeing her, or she was still at home. She could be ill, he supposed doubtfully. He hadn't thought of that.

Either way, he had nothing to lose by going and knocking at her door. If a neighbour saw him, he or she would probably assume he was a door-to-door salesman. Sheila Campbell was unlikely to hear about it, which was all that mattered to him.

He parked the car across the street, just in case anyone was watching. Then, thrusting open his door, he crossed the road and walked up the path to the white-painted front door.

He rang the bell, as he'd done a couple of days ago, and waited somewhat impatiently to see if anyone was home. He was half inclined to think the house was empty. There was no instantaneous rustle of someone coming to answer the door. But then his eye was caught by the awareness that someone had twitched the curtain of the window to one side of the door aside, and when he turned his head he found Helen staring at him from the other side of the glass.

She looked as shocked as he was, probably more so, and she continued to stare at him until he gestured for her to come and open the door. She hesitated, clearly weighing the odds of what he wanted against what would obviously be her mother's disapproval, and then drew back from the window out of his sight.

It seemed to take for ever for her to cross what he knew from previous experience was the sitting room and cover the short distance between there and the front door. But finally she opened the door, albeit reluctantly, hanging onto the handle as if she had no intention of letting him inside.

'Hi.' Milos managed to eject a cheerful inconsequence into his voice. 'Remember me?'

Helen's lips tightened. 'Of course.'

She was still wearing the faded jeans, this time teamed with a white tee shirt. Milos had to drag his eyes away from the pert nipples clearly etched against the cloth, reminding himself severely of why he was here.

'You're not at college today,' he said inanely, and she cast him a pitying look.

'Obviously not,' she said, proving she wasn't intimidated. 'What do you want, Mr Stephanides? I've got a lot of revision to do.'

'May I come in?'

That wasn't what he'd intended to say and he wasn't surprised when she shook her head. 'My mother's not here,' she said. 'She works half-days at the supermarket. If you come back about half past two, she should be home by then.'

Milos put out a hand to support himself on the wall beside the door, brows arching when she drew back in alarm. But, 'It's you I came to see, Helen,' he said, ignoring her reaction. 'Your father wanted me to talk to you. He'd very much like for you to forgive him.'

'I bet he would.' Her words echoed her mother's bitterness, but he sensed there was a reluctance in the sharp denial. 'My father doesn't care about me. He only cares about his new wife. He severed any hope of us being a family when he walked out on us.'

Milos sighed. 'He walked out on your mother; not on you.'

'And you think that excuses him?'

'No—'

'Because I have to tell you, I think what he did was pretty damn rotten.'

'I agree.' Milos didn't know all the ins and outs of the story, but he could see that from this girl's point of view her father's behaviour did seem unforgivable. 'But that doesn't alter your relationship to him. He's still your father. He still loves you.'

'Yeah, right.'

'He does. And, you know, he has tried to get in touch with you, but your mother has blocked him every time.'

Helen pursed her lips. 'So this is your real agenda, is it? To persuade me that he's not the villain I imagined him to be?'

Milos hesitated. If he said yes and she threw him out, he'd have lost any advantage he'd gained by coming here. On the other hand, if he said no, what other excuse could he offer for this visit? He was attracted to her, sure, but he couldn't tell her that. She was far too young for him.

Wasn't she?

Sighing, he said, 'I've told you, I'm on holiday.' He was actually on business, but he didn't think that would win him any favours. 'Your father suggested looking you up. Where's the harm in that? I've told you, he wants to mend bridges. If that's impossible, then so be it.'

'It is.'

She was adamant, her soft cheeks flushed with hectic colour. He found himself wanting to touch her skin, to run his fingertips over her warm flesh. She was so sure, so strong, yet so unconsciously vulnerable, he was entranced by her innocence.

She had no idea what she was doing to him as she stood so defiantly in the doorway.

A less—*arrogant* man, he decided, would back off at this point, but he didn't. Milos told himself he still believed he could change her mind in time, but that wasn't the real reason he wanted to see her again. She enchanted him; she intrigued him. He told himself he just wanted to see her smile—at him.

'Poli kala,' he said ruefully. 'I tried.' He glanced up and down the street as if preparing to leave and then came to what would prove to be a fatal decision. 'Look, I understand you have work to do right now, but won't you at least let me buy you a drink this evening?'

'Milos?'

Helen was speaking to him and he realised that for a few minutes he'd completely lost the plot. The memories of his trip to England were both vivid and painful, and it was hard to separate the present and the past.

CHAPTER NINE

'ARE you all right?'

Helen had taken a step closer, but when Milos's eyes focussed on hers she beat a hasty retreat. He realised she had been concerned about him and guessed, for a couple of minutes there, he hadn't heard a word she'd said.

'*Mia khara.* I'm fine,' he said swiftly, raking back his hair and feeling the dampness on his forehead. *Theos*, he must not let her get him rattled. His equilibrium was in danger of being shattered, particularly when his eyes were drawn to the dusky hollow between her breasts.

Trying to remember how he'd planned to deal with this, he said tersely, 'You didn't contact me again after you left the hotel.'

Helen's eyes widened and he didn't blame her. That was not something he'd planned to say. Nevertheless, he resented the fact that those dark-fringed violet eyes looked as innocent as if she had nothing on her conscience. She must suspect what he was thinking, he thought tensely. However she tried to play this, he hadn't got it wrong.

But, 'Contact you?' she echoed, as if the thought had never occurred to her. 'Why would I want to do that?'

'It's what men and women usually do after they've been to bed together,' he snapped irritably, his temper rekindling. 'Don't pretend—don't pretend what happened between us meant nothing to you. Or are you going to try and tell me it wasn't the first time you'd made love?'

Helen quivered. It was the first indication he'd touched a nerve and he waited expectantly for her response. 'I'd be foolish to do that,' she said at last, breathing deeply. 'But you were married. Did you expect me not to care?'

A pulse began to throb in Milos's temple. 'I have told you,' he said tightly. 'I was already separated from my wife when I made the trip to England.' He paused. 'But that reminds me of something you said earlier: when exactly did you speak to Eleni? I'd be interested to hear.'

Helen caught her lower lip between her teeth and Milos was beginning to wonder if she'd made the whole thing up when she spoke again. 'She phoned the hotel,' she said, totally confounding him, and he could only stare at her in disbelief.

'What hotel?'

'Well, duh.' She imitated Melissa's laconic way of mocking him. 'How many hotels did you stay at?'

Milos blinked. 'You mean the hotel where we—'

'Where you seduced me?' She flashed him a bitter smile. 'Yeah, that'd be right.'

'But how could she?' Milos couldn't take it in. 'She didn't know where I was staying.'

'Then someone must have told her,' said Helen practically. 'I don't suppose it was a secret, was it?'

Milos shook his head. 'When?' he asked, ignoring her question. 'When did she phone?'

'Can't you guess?' Helen's voice was flat now. 'You may remember, you'd gone into the bathroom to—to get rid of the evidence. She was very surprised when I answered your phone.'

'And what did you tell her?'

'Well, I didn't expose your dirty little secret,' said Helen with a grimace. 'Though I imagine she had her suspicions. Was that why you got a divorce?'

Milos's lips curled. 'Please,' he said. 'I've told

you how it was with Eleni and me. There was no love lost on either side.'

'That wasn't my impression.' Helen was sceptical.

'I don't care what your impression was,' he answered, his mind filled with the images of that evening at his hotel. He remembered going into the bathroom, to dispose of what had evidently proved to be a faulty condom. He remembered turning on the shower and sluicing his overheated body with cold water. He even remembered thinking Helen might like to join him. But when he'd come out of the bathroom, she'd gone.

'So why didn't you stay and tell me this?' he demanded now. 'Why didn't you ask me about Eleni, instead of running away like a spoilt child?'

'Because that's what I was,' she retorted. 'A child, anyway. And when she told me that you'd come to England, not for a holiday, as you'd said, but to get me to change my mind about my father, I knew the suspicions Mum had had about your motives were right.' She blew out a breath. 'Though why you thought seducing me would make me feel more sympathetic towards Sam, I can't imagine.'

'I didn't seduce you!' Milos couldn't prevent an

oath. 'So that's why you refused to speak to me again.'

'Among other things.' Helen sounded weary now. 'I felt sorry for your wife. She sounded really nice. I remember I made some excuse about us going out for dinner and you forgetting something. I told her you were just in the bathroom, but she didn't want to disturb you.'

'I can believe that!' Milos was furious. 'That woman had manipulation off to a fine art. She was lying, Helen. If she let you think I'd betrayed her, she was lying. You should have asked her whose bed she was sleeping in that night. I can guarantee it wouldn't have been her own.'

'And that excuses what you did?'

'I never said that.'

'No, but it did prove that you and my father were one of a kind.'

'No!' Milos swore again. 'Sam knew nothing about it. He still doesn't. He'd have killed me if he'd suspected what I'd done.'

'Chalk one up for my father, then.' Helen was derisive.

Milos sighed. 'He trusted me and I betrayed him.'

'And he betrayed my mother,' she countered. 'That makes you fairly even in my book.'

Milos lifted his shoulders helplessly. 'It wasn't quite the same.'

'No. Sam got a divorce and married Maya.'

'I meant, our—relationship; affair; whatever you want to call it—was too short.'

'And whose fault was that?'

'Well, it wasn't mine.' Milos ignored her attempt to deny his words and hastened on. 'I tried to see you again, Helen. You know I did. But you hid behind that gorgon of a mother of yours, and I had to get back to Greece.'

'How convenient!'

'It wasn't convenient at all,' said Milos harshly. 'I didn't know Eleni had been filling your head with lies. And I had a job to do, people that depended on me for their livelihood. As far as I was concerned, you'd made it pretty obvious you wanted nothing more to do with me.'

'Well, it's too late now.' Helen caught her tongue between her teeth and gave a little shiver—of what? Remorse? Regret? She moistened her lips. 'It's a pity you didn't tell me the truth at the beginning. It would have saved—'

She broke off abruptly, almost as if she was afraid she'd said too much, and Milos frowned. 'It would have saved—what?' he prompted, feeling as if he was on the brink of learning something significant. He took an involuntary step towards her. 'Helen—'

'I think this is the coffee you ordered,' she said quickly, once again taking his thoughts in an entirely different direction. He turned with some impatience to see the housekeeper stepping carefully onto the veranda with a tray.

'*Theos!*' His frustration was almost crippling and he had to force himself not to take his anger out on the old woman. 'Just put it on the table,' he ordered shortly, in his own language, and Andrea bowed her greying head in nervous submission.

'*Afto ineh ola, kirieh,*' she asked, giving Helen a hasty once over as she spoke.

Milos tamped down his irritation. '*Ineh mia khara, efkharisto.*' That's fine, thanks. His smile reassured her. '*Tipoteh alo.*'

The old woman returned his smile and, with another brief glance at his companion, she left them alone. As Milos had expected, Helen took the interruption as a way of evading continuing their discussion, and, contenting himself with the thought that she couldn't avoid him for ever, Milos let her get away with it.

She was obviously waiting for him to suggest

she take charge of the coffee, and when he didn't she approached the table herself. It was apparently the lesser of two evils, and, seating herself on one of the wicker chairs, she picked up the pot.

'Cream and sugar?' she asked politely, making a mockery of the ceremony, and Milos wanted to haul her up out of the chair and force her to finish what she'd been going to say.

'As it comes,' he said stiffly, watching as she poured some of the thick, aromatic beverage into a thin porcelain cup. But he couldn't help taking pleasure from the fact that her hand shook as she handed it to him.

He noticed that, although she poured herself some coffee, she didn't drink it. Instead, she took one of the honey-soaked pastries from the plate the housekeeper had provided, breaking the flaky sweet between her fingers, attempting to bring the crumbling morsel to her mouth.

Milos had sworn to himself that she wasn't going to distract him again, but his stomach lurched as her tongue swept out to rescue an errant crumb from her lower lip. There was something distinctly sensual in the way she was enjoying the pastry, and he set his cup back on the tray with a growing feeling of impotence.

As if sensing his frustrated regard, however, she finished the pastry and got to her feet again. Then, as if indifferent to his presence, she walked past him to the steps above the pool where she had been standing earlier.

'Did you mean what you said?' she asked, over her shoulder. 'About me taking a dip in the pool?'

Milos stifled a groan, and then, his jaw clenching, he said, 'If that's what pleases you.'

'It would please me if you would take me back to your parents' villa. But as I'm here...' She turned back to look at the pool again. 'Unfortunately, I didn't bring my swimsuit.'

'And that's a problem?'

He couldn't resist the taunt, but she'd had it her own way for far too long.

'Not for you, perhaps,' she said tersely, and he was pleased to see he'd disconcerted her. 'I'm not used to taking off my clothes in front of strange men.'

'Nor am I,' he remarked mildly and saw the way her lips compressed.

'Nor in front of strange women,' she retorted. 'I have a little more self-respect these days.'

The barb in the tail of the sentence didn't escape him, but he had no desire to cut their time together short. He nodded towards the row of wooden cabanas at the end of the pool deck. 'I think you'll find everything you need in there.'

Doubt momentarily crossed her sun-kissed features, but then she kicked off her high heels and started down the stone steps. She glanced back at him once, and he despised himself for the rush of emotion he felt when she half smiled at him. *Theos*, this wasn't supposed to be a pleasure trip. Here he was, humouring her, when he knew she was deliberately evading his questions.

Yet as he watched her descend the steps their fractured past was not the first thing he thought of. Her skirt swung about her long legs and he knew he couldn't wait to see her in one of the skimpy suits Rhea kept here for her own use. But sooner or later she was going to have to answer his questions, he assured himself. All he had to do was exercise a little patience, and there was no law that said he couldn't enjoy the process.

She emerged from the largest cabana a few minutes later. He'd half expected her to have second thoughts when she saw the swimsuits, but she evidently thought a swim could buy her a little more time.

The suit she'd chosen was a dark blue and white

outfit, its close-fitting top barely skimming her midriff, the bikini briefs cut high on her hip. Faint colour, which couldn't be blamed on the sun, tinged her cheeks when she found him waiting for her, but she swiftly moved to the side of the pool and executed a perfect dive into the water.

Milos was impressed. It was soon obvious that she was a strong swimmer. Instead of surfacing after the dive, she swam an impressive distance underwater before her head appeared again.

Milos was relieved to see her. Even though he'd been sure she was all right, it was good to have his confidence restored. He watched her strike out strongly for the other end of the pool before somersaulting a turn and starting back. Her body cleaved surely through the water, her arms rising and falling in an almost hypnotic rhythm.

Despite himself, Milos descended the steps so that he was in her line of vision. She couldn't help but see him waiting for her, his feet parted, his arms folded across his chest. If it was a gesture of defence, he was unaware of it. He wanted to disconcert her, to let her feel the insistent pull she was having on his senses.

Helen ignored him, however. When she reached the end where he was standing, she simply repeated the somersault she'd turned at the other end of the pool and swam back the way she'd come.

Milos was infuriated. The heat around the pool was palpable and he cast an irritated glance towards the sun. He must be crazy, he thought, exposing himself to possible sunstroke just to make a point. She was determined to ignore him, it seemed. He would have to think of something else.

He had already unbuttoned his shirt and pulled it free of his jeans before he acknowledged she was driving him crazy. Kicking off the boots he'd originally worn to ride the Harley, he unzipped his jeans and pushed them down his legs. Kicking the jeans off, too, he hooked his thumbs into his boxers. And then hesitated. In deference to his guest's sensibilities, Milos didn't go any further. As she swam steadily towards him he dived into the water, emerging only inches from her stroking arms.

The splash he made caused her to lose her rhythm. She flailed about for a few moments before she realised what he'd done. Treading water, she stared indignantly at him, almost as if he had no right to use the pool, before turning abruptly towards the steps.

'Wait!'

Milos caught her arm as she would have swum away from him. She struggled for a moment before realising she was wasting her time and Milos took advantage of her acquiescence to bring her back to him. He'd let her go when he chose, not her, he thought grimly, but already his flesh was betraying him.

He couldn't help but be aware of how soft her skin felt beneath his fingers. Even the slight pressure he was exerting was bringing the dusky blush of colour to a limb that was as smooth and fine as silk. When she looked up at him, her water-spiked lashes caused her eyes to shimmer so that he couldn't see what she was thinking. But he certainly knew what her nearness was doing to him.

'What do you want?' she demanded, and he wondered if he only imagined the faint tremor in her voice. Then, with a suddenly indrawn breath, 'Are you wearing anything at all?'

Her words were so unexpected that Milos felt a reluctant grin tugging at the corners of his mouth. 'What kind of a question is that?'

'A fairly simple one,' she retorted, sweeping back her wet hair with her free hand. 'I didn't see you go into the cabana.'

'That's because I didn't,' Milos acknowledged, noticing how the water had darkened her blonde hair so that it clung to her head like a golden cap. 'Does it matter?'

He could see that she wanted to object, but she was determined not to give him any advantage. 'Not to me,' she replied tightly, using her legs to ensure she kept a distance between them. 'It's not as if it's something I haven't seen before.'

Milos resented that. And whatever she said, he knew she wasn't as blasé about his proximity as she would like him to believe. Nevertheless, he was still prepared to be generous. 'All right,' he said. 'But just to reassure you, I can tell you I'm not totally naked.'

'Big deal.' She made a careless gesture. 'But just for the record, I don't care.' She shrugged. 'And you have to admit, it's just the sort of stunt you would pull.'

'So you think I'm lying?'

'I didn't say that.'

'But you think it,' he snapped, suppressing the urge to shake her. He took a deep breath. 'You can trust me. I'm not lying.'

'Whatever.'

The careless dismissal was humiliating. And

when she turned her head away, looking resignedly towards the steps, his temper snapped. He'd been more than patient so far, he assured himself. But she was determined to provoke him.

Without really thinking of the consequences, he jerked her towards him. Wrapping one of his legs about both of hers, he brought her into intimate contact with his lower body. Then, scowling down at her, he said, 'Now do you believe me?'

He'd taken her by surprise and her initial response was to wrap a startled arm about his shoulders to keep her balance. Her fingers clutched wildly at the hair at the back of his neck, her slim body curling instinctively into his.

He felt his own arousal only seconds before she felt it, too. Tiny globules of moisture were trembling on the slopes of her breasts that were only inches below his gaze. She was so close in fact, that he could feel the betraying thrust of her nipples nudging his chest, the taut fabric of the vest top only adding to the intimacy.

Suddenly, he wanted to see her naked. His thumbs itched to hook inside the sexy top and pull it forcefully to her waist. He knew the bikini briefs would offer no obstruction. It would be a simple matter to dispose of them in the same way.

He tried to steady his roiling senses. This was not why he'd brought her here, he reminded himself. Getting overheated wasn't going to solve anything.

But holding her like this, feeling her limbs twisting frantically against him, brought back memories of why he'd acted so uncharacteristically all those years ago. He'd never been the kind of man to use sex indiscriminately, and it was only the raw attraction she'd aroused in him that had caused him to act in such a reckless way. From the moment they'd met, she'd exerted a powerful pull on his senses, and making love with her had been as natural as breathing to him.

With thoughts like these filling his head, he should have resisted going any further. A saner man—a more calculating man—would have used the situation to his advantage and asked her outright who Melissa's father was. In her present state of agitation, he doubted she'd have had time to fabricate an answer, and even if she'd denied his involvement her reaction would have given her away.

Or so he believed.

But instead, when she grabbed a handful of his hair and yanked his head back, all he saw was red. With her hot breath panting in his ear and the spaghetti straps falling down her arms and pulling her top perilously close to total exposure, all he could think about was retaliation. The uncontrollable rush of blood to his groin was the final straw and all thought of letting her go became academic.

'*Ya Theos*, keep still,' he muttered, making a futile attempt to control his emotions. But when he looked into her flushed face, he was lost. With her soft lips parted and a hectic blush rising in her cheeks, she was irresistible, and he knew it. With a groan of defeat, he gave in to the driving need inside him and, bending his head, he captured her lips with his.

CHAPTER TEN

HELEN'S lips parted beneath his, and, moving his hand to the back of her neck, Milos deepened the kiss. Pushing his tongue between her teeth, he completely forgot that it was only his efforts that were keeping them afloat. Without anything to keep them buoyant, they sank to the bottom of the pool, their mouths still glued together.

It was an incredible experience. Milos knew he had never felt anything like the dizzying exultation that filled his head when Helen's fingers curled around his nape, denoting her submission, and not even the buzzing in his ears, reminding him of his lack of oxygen, prevented an urgent surge of need from sweeping over him.

His hand trailed down her body, grazing the hard peaks of her breasts before fastening on the slender bones of her pelvis. He parted his legs, bringing her more fully into him, letting her feel the turgid pressure of his erection. He rubbed himself against her, but his lungs were labouring for air, and, judging by Helen's submissive behaviour, she wasn't about to save them. With a feeling of regret, he pushed down with his feet and sent them rising steadily to the surface.

Within seconds she had torn herself away from him. Splashing wildly through the water, she made for the steps out of the pool. And, because Milos took rather longer to recover, she'd stumbled out of the water before he could stop her.

She paused once, bending forward as if the effort had defeated her. She was coughing, her hands braced on her knees, trying to suck air into her burning lungs. Then she turned to give him a tortured look.

'You—crazy—fool,' she got out with difficulty, her voice made husky by her distress. 'What in God's name did you think you were doing?'

Milos took a deep breath and swam smoothly to the side. 'Well, not trying to drown you,' he said wearily as she retreated up the steps. 'Stop panicking. No harm has been done.'

'Just—stay away from me,' she told him unsteadily, but he could tell from the way her eyes flicked to the row of cabanas that she was undecided what to do next. Safety might lie in the villa, but her clothes were in the cabana.

Spreading his arms wide, to indicate she had nothing to fear from him, Milos climbed out of the pool. Unlike her, apparently, he was still suffering the after-effects of that kiss, and like her he took a few moments to steady his breathing.

'I'm sorry,' he said at last, though it pained him to say it. 'I suppose you think that shouldn't have happened.'

'Damn right!' Her voice quivered, but he could see she was determined not to back down.

Milos lifted his shoulders. 'Then you shouldn't have provoked me.'

Helen gave an indignant snort. 'Because I asked if you were wearing—swimming gear?' she exclaimed hotly.

'No. Because you wouldn't believe me,' he retorted smoothly. 'And as you can see, I am adequately covered.'

It wasn't the most sensible thing to say in his present position. When her eyes dropped automatically to his boxer shorts, his treacherous body couldn't help but respond.

And she noticed.

'You—you're shameless,' she said, winding protective arms about her midriff. 'Do—do you ever think of anything but sex?'

Milos stared at her in disbelief. *Theos*, he knew he hadn't imagined the instinctive response he'd felt in those moments before he'd been forced to push up to the surface of the pool. She'd been just as involved as he'd been, and it infuriated him that she could stand there and pretend that what had happened had been all his doing.

But what was new?

'You—amuse me, do you know that?' he demanded between his teeth, although what she really did to him didn't bear description. 'You deluded yourself that you had no part in our love-making fourteen years ago, and you're doing the same again now.'

'No, it's you who is deluding himself,' she told him swiftly. 'I didn't want to come here, Milos. You made me. And now I'd like to go back.'

'I'll just bet you would,' he muttered, barely audibly, as he bounded up the remainder of the steps and wrapped his arm about her waist. Then, for the third time that day, he damned his soul by covering her trembling mouth with his.

There was a moment when he thought she was going to resist. Her hands came up and dug painfully into his shoulders, but her anger didn't last. When his tongue invaded her mouth, filling that hot, wet cavern with a greedy hunger, she uttered a helpless little moan of submission. Then, her fingers spread and lingered, gripping his arms now as if to save herself from falling.

He didn't attempt to hide his response to her eagerness. A hot lust was pounding through his veins and the memory of what they had once shared was like a fever in his blood. He was blind to everything but the knowledge that he wanted her again. He wanted to taste her, to tempt her, to show her that what had been between them was by no means over.

With a groan vibrating in his chest, he hooked his thumbs into the vest top, pulling it down far enough so that he could lick the moist hollow between her breasts. She tasted so good, her heat surging to meet his tongue despite the pool-induced chill of her skin. She melted under his hands, swaying helplessly against him. She was making sensuous little sounds, too, her fingers moving restlessly into his hair.

He knew she was no longer in control of her emotions. Milos felt a surge of satisfaction at the thought of how easily she'd succumbed to his demands. She might hate him later, but right now she was breathing heavily, her limbs soft and trembling against his.

His eyes dropped to her breasts and, bending his head, he pushed the stretchy fabric low enough for him to take one engorged nipple into his mouth. He rolled it against his tongue, hearing the whimpers of pleasure she was making, and contemplated how she would react if he slipped his hands inside the bikini briefs.

But before he could act on it, before he could do anything more than press her even closer to his throbbing erection, the sound of spinning rotor blades rent the air. They were accompanied by the roar of powerful engines, and Milos needed no crystal ball to know what they presaged.

He swore then, in his own language, but the words he used were scarcely adequate to describe his frustration. There was no longer any opportunity to expose more of Helen's delectable body, and, while common sense might applaud that reality, his emotional needs were fairly screaming their regrets.

Reluctantly, he pulled her top up over her breasts and placed his hands on her shoulders. Somehow, he had to rescue this situation before the pilot of his helicopter stepped out of the aircraft. It wasn't going to be easy with Helen gazing up at him in wide, uncomprehending inquiry. There was so much he wanted to do with her, so much he still had to say. And now, *skata*, it was too late. Too late, especially, to tell her how she made him feel.

'I'm sorry,' he said, and he knew at once that he'd said the wrong thing.

'You're sorry,' she echoed, and as the words took root he saw the dreamy expression draining out of her eyes and something else, something much less attractive, taking its place. 'Oh, yes. You're very good at being sorry after the event.'

'You don't understand—'

'Oh, I think I do.'

'My helicopter is here,' he said, through clenched teeth. 'It's just arrived. Didn't you hear it? It's come to fly me to Athens for the conference.'

'Where's Milos?'

Helen's lips tightened. How ironic that that should be the first question Melissa asked when she and Rhea got back to the villa at San Rocco. Not *Where have you been?* Or *Did you have a good time?* Just *Where's Milos?* As if he was the person her daughter most wanted to see.

'He's getting ready to leave for Athens,' Helen

replied, amazed that she could answer the question so coolly. 'He was—we were at Vassilios when his helicopter arrived.'

'His helicopter! Wow!' Melissa was impressed. She turned to Rhea, who was just behind her. 'Is it really *his* helicopter?'

'It belongs to the company,' said Rhea evenly, but Helen was aware that the girl's eyes were on her, not on Melissa. 'It's more convenient than a plane.'

'Cool!' Melissa's eyes sparkled. 'imagine that: having a helicopter you can use any time you feel like it.'

'Anyway, he said you knew all about it,' Helen put in, addressing herself to Rhea. 'He sends his apologies for not saying goodbye.'

Rhea nodded, her eyes still thoughtful. 'He's attending a conference about reducing oil pollution,' she said absently. Then, 'Did he have time to bring you back?'

'No. Stelios did that.'

But Helen didn't want to think about that now. It was enough to know that she could still smell the pool water on her body, could still feel the possessive touch of Milos's hands, Milos's mouth. What must he have thought when she'd scuttled into the cabana and pulled on her clothes without even taking a shower? What was she supposed to make of the look on his face when he was forced to bid her a public goodbye?

Shaking off the remembrance, she tried to speak casually. 'I—er—I suppose we should be going, too.'

'But we haven't had lunch,' objected Melissa at once, turning to Rhea for support. 'You said Marisa would have everything ready.'

'And I meant it.' Rhea seemed to gather herself, putting out a hand towards Helen as if in apology. 'My mother's housekeeper will be most offended if you deny her the chance to show off her culinary skills,' she insisted. But Helen was still left wondering if she truly wanted them to stay.

'Well...'

She hesitated, and Melissa took the chance to speak again. 'Come on, Mum,' she persisted. 'It's not as if you've got anything else to do.'

Which was true, Helen admitted silently. Now that Milos had left the island, she didn't have to worry about him turning up unexpectedly. She ought to have been feeling relieved that he was gone. But all she really felt was defeated.

'All right,' she said at last, earning herself a delighted whoop from Melissa. Her father was expecting them to stay, after all, and it would save a lot of unnecessary explanations.

And, in spite of her reluctance, the visit was not so bad. She'd expected to find it hard to talk to Milos's sister, but she didn't. The girl had evidently decided it wasn't Helen's fault that her brother had deserted them, and over a meal of stuffed vine leaves, a crisp green salad, and a sticky sweet dessert, she made an effort to be friendly.

She told Helen about the course she was taking at college and her plans to set up her own interior-decorating business as soon as she graduated. Her father had agreed to finance her for the first year, and Helen thought how lucky Rhea was to have such loving and supportive parents.

It made her wonder if she'd have felt differently about her own situation if she hadn't cut her father out of her life. Would he have recommended that she marry Richard if she'd confided her pregnancy to him? Of course, her mother had been concerned about what other people were going to think when they discovered Helen was unmarried and expecting a baby. She'd never really got over the gossip that had ensued when Sam had walked out.

Of course, if her father hadn't walked out, Helen would never have met Milos Stephanides. She'd never have found herself pregnant with a baby whose father's identity she'd kept secret even from her mother...

'Where are you going?'

Sheila Campbell turned from the television when Helen appeared in the sitting-room doorway. She was obviously surprised to see her daughter dressed and ready to go out when she'd said nothing about having a date earlier in the day.

'I'm going to meet Sally at the coffee bar,' said Helen quickly, mouthing the first lie that came into her head. She had thought of making Richard, her current boyfriend, her excuse, but her mother was bound to ask Richard about it later on and she couldn't have that.

'Sally? Sally who?' Sheila frowned, and Helen wished her mother were not so interested in everything she did.

'Sally Phillips,' she said, hoping she sounded convincing. 'You don't know her. She's in my English tutor group.'

'Oh?' Sheila shrugged and turned back to the television. 'Well, don't forget it's a school night. I shall expect you home before half past ten.'

'Oh, Mum!' Helen gave a resigned sigh. 'I'm not a child, you know.'

'But you are still a student. And I don't have time to haul you out of bed in the morning.' She sniffed. 'In any case, I thought you told me you preferred to see Richard at weekends.'

'I do.' Helen was indignant. 'And I'm not meeting Richard Shaw. As I say, I'm going to the coffee bar. Is that all right?'

'Do I have a choice?' Sheila was dismissive. 'Oh, go on. Enjoy your evening. But don't you miss the last bus home.'

'I won't,' said Helen guiltily, wondering if Milos would bring her back to her door. Well, to the end of the street, anyway, she amended, feeling again the frisson of excited anticipation she'd felt since she'd agreed to have a drink with him.

They were meeting in the bar of his hotel and Helen wondered if she'd been entirely wise in agreeing to that. But at least she could be reasonably sure she wouldn't see anyone she knew at the Cathay Intercontinental. The rates there were phenomenally high. Or so she'd always believed.

She just hoped that what she was wearing wouldn't look totally out of place. She would have liked to have worn her new slip dress and the suede jacket she'd been saving up for for ages, but that would have been foolish and she knew it. The last thing she wanted was for her mother to become suspicious, so the tight-fitting jeans and black parka would have to do. But she had put on the purple silk shirt her mother had bought her for her last birthday under the parka, away from Sheila's prying gaze.

Which made her feel really sneaky and she didn't like it. She was no better than her father, she thought, keeping secrets from her mother.

But when she walked into the foyer of the Cathay Intercontinental and found Milos standing near the entrance waiting for her, she was selfishly glad she had deceived her. He looked so good in his dark suit and turtle-neck sweater, and she could hardly believe this gorgeous hunk was waiting for her.

But he was. He came towards her at once, his dark disturbing eyes making her whole body feel hot and alive. She tried to tell herself it was natural for him to look at a woman in that way. But there was something intensely personal in the melting heat of his gaze.

'Hi,' he said softly, and, although he made no attempt to touch her, Helen felt as if his hands had stroked over every inch of her skin. 'I'm glad you came. I wondered if you would. I was afraid your mother would change your mind.'

'She doesn't know I'm here.'

Her denial was instinctive, and she thought how pathetic she must sound to a man like him. Dear God, he would think she didn't have a mind or a will of her own. Or that she was scared to tell her mother something she knew she wouldn't like.

Milos's lips compressed. 'So where does she think you are?' he inquired, and Helen shifted somewhat unhappily beneath his curious stare.

'At the coffee bar,' she said quickly. Then, 'I suppose you think I'm stupid, not telling her where I was going.'

Milos shook his head. 'I think it was probably very wise,' he said drily. 'I got the distinct impression that your mother didn't like me.'

Helen gave a rueful smile. 'She has reason, don't you think?'

'Because I've invited you to have a drink with me?' he asked. 'Surely that's not so unforgivable.

I want to get to know you better. I'm hoping we can be friends.'

Friends?

Helen let that go, but she was under no illusion that her mother would ever allow her to be friends with a man who worked for her father. Still, it was nice to know that he didn't have an ulterior motive, and she was woman enough to feel flattered that he should want to see her again.

'Let me take your coat,' he said now, and although Helen suspected she should keep it on—just in case—she obediently unfastened the zip. Besides, glancing about her at all the glamorously clad women entering and leaving the lobby, she could see that her parka was very much out of place. At least her shirt was new and fashionable, its deep vee neckline and string ties at the waist giving her a spurious look of maturity.

Her coat was deposited with the cloakroom attendant and then Milos directed her into the cocktail bar that adjoined the famous restaurant. A waiter, recognising her escort, immediately found them a corner table, and Milos made sure she was seated comfortably and then ordered champagne.

With hindsight, Helen had realised that she shouldn't have drunk any champagne. She wasn't old enough to drink alcohol, for one thing, and, for another, she'd never tried anything but beer before. And then only at a party when she would have looked a prude to refuse it. But she hadn't liked the taste on that occasion and had dumped most of the bottle down the loo.

Champagne, as she discovered, was different. It was much sweeter, and the bubbles fizzed pleasantly on her tongue. In addition to which, it seemed to give her confidence and she found herself chattering on about the subjects she was taking to A level, and her ambitions for the future, with an uncharacteristic lack of reticence.

In no time at all, it seemed, it was eight o'clock, and when Milos invited her to stay and have dinner with him it would have been churlish to refuse. Besides, she didn't want to. She liked being with Milos; she liked the envious female eyes that were cast in her direction. But most of all she liked it that he made her feel like a woman, an attractive woman that he was proud to be with.

They struck a snag when Milos summoned the waiter and asked if he had a table in the restaurant. The man was most apologetic, but the earliest he could accommodate them was at half past nine, which Helen insisted was much too late. If, as she was considering, she intended telling her mother where she'd been after the event, she had to get home at an acceptable time.

'Send the head waiter over, would you?' Milos asked now, politely but a little autocratically, Helen thought, and almost immediately the *maître d'* presented himself, looking decidedly embarrassed at having to disappoint an apparently important guest.

'We knew you were staying in the hotel, Mr Stephanides,' he said, pressing his hands together a little diffidently. 'But you did not reserve a table, sir, and one of our other guests, Prince Halil Mohammad—' he said the other man's name with some deference '—made an unexpected late reservation for himself and his entourage to dine in the restaurant.' He threw up his hands in apology. 'I am so sorry, sir.'

Milos was regarding him coldly, and Helen was feeling almost sorry for the man himself when he said, 'I suppose you would not consider dining in your suite, Mr Stephanides. I would be happy to arrange for you to be served immediately. With the management's compliments, of course.'

Helen's cheeks turned pink then. She knew what the man was saying was reasonable. If, as he said,

Milos did have a suite of rooms, then it wasn't as if he was suggesting they had dinner in Milos's bedroom.

But before she could make any comment, Milos intervened. 'I think not,' he said curtly, obviously expecting her to object. 'I suppose I'll have to make other arrangements.'

'I wouldn't mind.'

Helen could hardly believe she'd said the words. But the knowledge that to refuse would make her look like the kid she was had her accepting the *maître d'*'s suggestion with apparent ease.

'You're sure?'

Milos was looking at her now, and she felt the frisson of excitement she'd felt earlier stirring inside her again. It might be the champagne, but she didn't regret coming here. This was so much more thrilling than spending an evening watching Richard getting progressively wasted.

So, 'I'm sure,' she said, hoping she wouldn't regret her recklessness. 'Thank you.'

CHAPTER ELEVEN

MILOS'S apartments were on the top floor of the hotel. Helen supposed it was a penthouse suite, with double-panelled doors opening into a large sitting room. Other doors opened from the sitting room, one of them obviously being his bedroom, and she shivered a little uneasily as the heavy doors closed behind them.

They had ordered downstairs and the waiter had assured them they wouldn't have to wait long for their food. Looking about her, Helen saw the table standing in the bay of the window with some relief. Obviously it was quite common to be served in the apartment and she made a determined effort to relax.

'Would you like a drink while we wait?' Milos suggested as she hovered near the window. 'Some wine, perhaps. Or would you prefer some music?' He bent to a sophisticated sound system and moments later the rhythmic sound of Santana filled the room.

Helen turned, her lips parted. 'Oh, I love this,' she said, unable to prevent the automatic shift her body made to the music. 'Is it your CD?'

'It is, actually,' he said, coming towards her and holding out his arms. 'Do you want to dance?'

'Dance?' Helen's breath caught in her throat.

'Why not?' he asked, catching both her hands in his and drawing her forward into the hypnotic beat. 'Your body obviously wants to.'

Helen licked her lips. 'I've just—never done anything like this before,' she confessed.

'I know,' he said, making no attempt to pull her closer. 'But it's fun, isn't it?'

'Fun?' Helen's response was breathless. 'Yes. Yes, it is.'

'Good.'

The knock at the door interrupted them, and Helen couldn't exactly say she was sorry. Her legs had become increasingly shaky, and looking into Milos's dark eyes was making her weak.

The waiter wheeled a trolley into the apartment and started setting the table. Pristine white place mats gleamed against the dark wood, silver tableware glinted in the light from candles set in the middle of the table, and tall wineglasses of the finest crystal prepared the way for wines of both white and red.

Their first course—a mousse of crab and lobster—was served and the waiter stood back, waiting for Milos's instructions.

'We'll serve the rest ourselves,' Milos told him as the crisp crackle of notes changed hands, and moments later the doors closed again and they were alone.

Later, Helen could hardly remember how the food tasted. It could have been arsenic or ambrosia, she doubted she'd have noticed. With Milos sitting beside her, his knee brushing hers, serving her tiny morsels of what he was eating from his plate, she was too bemused to pay attention to her own food. She only knew she was floating several inches above the table for most of the meal, the sensuous rhythm of the music and the disturbing directness of Milos's gaze causing a sensation of elevation in the pit of her stomach.

After the meal was over, Helen needed to use the restroom, and she discovered that one of the doors that opened off the living room led into a luxuriously appointed vanity-cum-bathroom. Lamp lit mirrors lined the walls, inviting inspection of her appearance, while the marble bathroom adjoining was as big as the largest bedroom back home.

She availed herself of the facilities and then paused for a moment beside the row of mirrors, intrigued by her appearance. She almost looked beautiful, she thought, touching the hectic colour in her cheeks, noticing how soft her lips looked in the flattering light. She also noticed that, despite the fact that she was wearing a bra, her nipples were clearly outlined against the thin fabric of her shirt.

She crossed her arms over her chest and then let them fall again. Who was she kidding? she thought impatiently. If Milos was being unusually attentive to her it was because he'd promised her father he'd look after her. She shouldn't run away with the idea that he was attracted to her. He was just being friendly, that was all.

The trolley had disappeared when she emerged from the bathroom. Either the waiter had been summoned to remove it, or Milos had pushed it out into the corridor himself. The table was now empty of everything except the wine and their glasses, but Helen, who had tried to drink sparingly during the meal, determined not to have any more.

Milos was standing by the white marble fireplace when she re-entered the room, but Helen moved to the windows, to stand looking down at the lights of Knightsbridge sparkling thirty floors below. It was quite a view, even though a light rain had come to slick the pavements. It blurred the image, making her feel as if she were watching it through a mirror.

She was so absorbed that she got quite a shock when Milos put his hand on her shoulder. She'd been unaware of him coming to stand beside her, and the warm strength of his fingers caused a ripple of excitement in her stomach.

She turned towards him a little breathlessly, her agitation showing in the eyes she turned up to his lean face. Her lips parted in an unknowing invitation and she saw the way his eyes darkened as they identified her expression.

'*Signomi.* I'm sorry,' he said, his low voice with its distinctive accent like velvet on her skin. 'Did I frighten you?'

'You—startled me,' she amended, aware of the quickening beat of her heart. She nervously cleared her throat. 'I—er—I was admiring the view.'

'So was I,' he said softly, and her stomach wobbled at the realisation that he wasn't talking about the scene outside.

'Um—I suppose I should be going,' she said, half afraid of her own reaction to his words. He was only being polite, she told herself, trying to remember how she'd felt when he'd turned up on her doorstep. This man was not her friend, she reminded herself. Her mother would be horrified if she ever discovered that Helen had had dinner with him in his suite.

'Oh—you must stay and have coffee,' he protested now, nodding towards the sofa, and she saw the tray she hadn't noticed before residing on the low table close by. 'Come,' he added. 'Let us sit down. And don't worry about getting home. I've arranged for a car and driver to be available when we need them.'

Helen hesitated only a moment before doing as he suggested. But as she sank into the soft cushions she couldn't help wondering when he'd ordered a car. Had he intended her to have dinner with him all along?

It was a disturbing consideration and her teeth dug into her bottom lip as Milos seated himself beside her. What did she really know about this man? she asked herself uneasily. How did she know she could trust him?

Milos's weight depressed the cushions deeper than hers did, and she felt herself slipping closer. It took all her ingenuity to sustain a little space between them without his being aware of it. Or perhaps he was. She couldn't be sure.

'Will you...?'

He indicated the cups and Helen drew a deep breath and moved forward. There was a tall jug of coffee and another smaller one of cream, and two white porcelain cups that seemed almost transparent.

The delicacy of the operation was not lost on her, and Helen couldn't help her hand shaking as she lifted the pot and attempted to pour. Dear God, she was going to spill it all over the white linen cloth. Either that, or drop the pot on the fragile china.

She was aware of Milos watching her and her gaze was drawn irresistibly in his direction. Which was definitely a mistake. As she'd feared, the coffee cascaded over the side of the cup, filling the saucer and splashing hotly onto her jean-clad legs.

'Oh, shit!' she exclaimed, as much in pain as

frustration, and without hesitation Milos took the pot from her trembling fingers and replaced it on the tray.

'You're hurt,' he said roughly, snatching up a napkin and dabbing at the damp spots on her trousers. '*Theos*, this was all my fault. I shouldn't have been watching you.'

Helen would agree with that, but she couldn't let him take the blame for something that was really all her own doing. 'It wasn't your fault,' she insisted, pushing her hands over her knees in an effort to deflect his efforts. 'Really. I knew I was going to make a mess of it.'

Milos tossed the napkin onto the tray, his lips twitching with reluctant amusement. 'Well, you certainly did that,' he agreed, nodding at the stained tray cloth. 'Never mind. I'm not fond of English coffee anyway. So long as you're not burned, that's all that matters.'

'Oh, I'm all right,' she said ruefully, dragging her eyes from his. 'My—er—my jeans took the worst of it.'

Milos's eyes dropped to her knees and Helen's stomach did a nervous somersault. There was such a look of tenderness in his gaze and her limbs turned to liquid when he captured her hands in both of his.

'Are you sure?' he asked, and for a moment Helen hadn't the first idea what he was talking about. When he'd touched her shoulder earlier, she'd been startled by her reaction, but that was as nothing compared to the way she felt when he raised one of her hands to his lips. He bestowed a fleeting kiss on her knuckles before turning her hand over and caressing her palm. His thumb massaged the moist centre in a deliberately sensual motion and she felt the heat he was generating spreading to every extremity. It was an almost physical invasion and she hardly dared to identify its effect.

Her eyes had been drawn back to his, but now she tried to look away. She didn't want him to see how vulnerable she was, how easily he had breached barriers she had had years to erect.

She didn't understand it. She'd been Richard's girlfriend for almost two years and he'd never come close to arousing her in this way. Oh, they'd kissed and petted, of course they had, and just occasionally she'd been tempted to find out what all the fuss was about. But she'd always been in control of her emotions and Richard had known she didn't sleep around.

Yet now, the melting sensation in her stomach was causing all sorts of problems. There was a tightness in her breasts, a moistness between her legs, and the blood that had been pounding through her veins now seemed to have congealed just beneath her skin. She was hot and cold by turns, sweating one minute and shivering the next, while a wave of goose-bumps enveloped her in a rippling cloak of excitement.

She was beginning to realise how reckless she had been in coming here, yet she also knew Milos wouldn't do anything she didn't want him to. Despite her earlier doubts, she thought she could trust him. The trouble was, she didn't trust herself.

As if sensing her confusion, Milos chose that moment to release her hands. 'You are very sweet, *agape mou*,' he said, patting her knee with what she recognised was genuine affection. 'And so innocent,' he continued, looking into her flushed face. 'You make me feel things I shouldn't feel.'

Helen's lips parted. 'What things?' she asked naïvely, but she knew. She just wanted him to say them, to admit that she wasn't the only one who was feeling the intimacy between them.

'You don't want to know.'

'I do. I do.' She gazed up at him eagerly. 'Please; you have to tell me.' She paused and then added provocatively, 'Do you think I'm attractive?'

Dear God! Helen almost cringed then. Where had that come from? She'd thought the meal had banished the worst effects of the champagne from her system, but she'd been wrong. Terribly wrong.

Milos, however, chose to answer her. 'Yes,' he said softly. 'I find you very attractive.'

'Was that why you wanted to see me again?' In for a penny, in for a pound, thought Helen recklessly. 'I thought you wanted to talk about my father.'

'I did. I should,' he amended, a little roughly. 'But—we've talked about other things.'

'Me,' said Helen ruefully. 'Were you bored?'

'Very,' he said drily. 'That's why I asked you to have dinner with me.'

Helen bit her lip. 'You don't talk about yourself much, do you?' she ventured with a frown, and he shrugged.

'I *am* very boring,' he said flatly. 'And now I think I ought to take you home.'

Helen protested. 'It's early yet.' She glanced towards the sound system. 'Couldn't we play some more music? Maybe dance again?'

'I think not.'

'Why?'

Milos said something then that she thought wasn't very complimentary, but almost against his will, it seemed, he didn't get up from the sofa.

Instead, he hesitated only a moment before lifting his hand and slipping it under the hair at the back of her neck. His strong fingers first massaged and then gripped her nape, forcing her to look at him.

'You know exactly why I have to take you home,' he told her roughly. 'Why we have to put an end to this right now.'

Helen pressed her lips together. 'Because you're tired of me?' she asked ingenuously. 'Because you don't want to dance with me again?'

Milos's jaw hardened. 'That's not what I want to do, and you know it.'

Helen angled her neck beneath his hand. 'That sounds ominous.'

'Helen!' He spoke harshly. 'Don't make this any harder than it already is. You're just an eighteen-year-old student, while I—I'm not.'

She was actually seventeen, but Helen didn't

think this was a good time to say that. But it did explain why he'd offered her champagne.

'You're not old,' she said instead. 'And I'm not exactly inexperienced, you know.'

Milos breathed deeply. 'Where are you going with this?'

'Where do you want to go?'

She was being deliberately provocative, but she trembled when his fingers tightened on her nape.

He was going to kiss her, she thought unsteadily, hoping she wouldn't regret this. She wanted him to kiss her, she told herself. She wanted to have some point of reference so that when she let Richard kiss her again she'd be able to gauge which of them was the best.

But Milos didn't kiss her. He just stared at her with tormented eyes, and she felt herself shrinking beneath his dark disturbed gaze.

'I know you don't mean to be cruel,' he said grimly. 'But, Helen, this isn't a game. Whatever experience you think you've had, forget it. You're going to hate me if I take you at your word.'

'I'm not.' The protest burst from her, a need to reassure him now taking precedence over her own fears. 'I like you, Milos. And I thought you liked me. What could possibly be wrong with that?'

It was the last coherent moment she had. When Milos's lips touched hers, she forgot all about Richard, all about her parents, all about everything except the sensuous brush of his mouth against hers. Any thoughts of a rational nature were swiftly shattered by those featherlight caresses and the quivering they aroused inside her seemed to swell and expand until even her skin felt almost too brittle to contain it.

His mouth played with hers as his fingers had played with hers earlier. And, in no time at all, she was reaching for him, clutching the lapels of his suit jacket, giving herself up to the unimaginable pleasure of his kisses. She wasn't exactly sure what she wanted, but she wanted more, and it was her amateurish efforts to get close to him that changed the whole tenor of his embrace.

Muttering a groan, Milos's mouth fastened on hers, pressing her back against the cushions behind her. She felt the erratic pulse of his heart beating against hers as he deepened and lengthened the kiss, the unsteady brush of his hand against her breast as he sloughed off his jacket and loosened his tie.

Then his tongue was stroking over her lower lip, forcing its way between her teeth and into her mouth. Hot and wet, it was unbearably sexy, and Helen's senses went into overload. Ignoring the warning prick of her conscience, she sank lower on the cushions until Milos was practically lying on top of her.

Somehow the buttons of her shirt had become unfastened, making it easy for him to slide his hand inside. His strong fingers cupped her breast over her bra and that sensual caress caused an ache of desire to flower deep in her belly. Heat spread over her and through her, and when he bent his head lower and sucked her nipple through the cloth she couldn't prevent the convulsive cry that escaped her.

'Did I hurt you?' he asked at once, pushing himself up to look down at her, and she gave a violent shake of her head. 'You're sure?'

'I'm sure,' she assured him huskily, winding her arms around his neck. Then, shyly, 'Don't stop.'

Milos closed his eyes for a moment. 'I don't want to stop,' he admitted unevenly, and as he lowered himself onto her again she felt the insistent pressure of his erection hard against her stomach. 'But, this is crazy! *Theos*— I want to make love with you, Helen. And it's tearing me up because that's not going to happen.'

'Why not?'

She heard herself ask the question, but she didn't regret it. This was so different from anything she'd shared with Richard that in her present frame of mind she found it hard to believe it could possibly be wrong.

'Because we hardly know one another,' he told her roughly. 'And, quite honestly, I can't imagine your mother allowing us to see one another again.'

Helen couldn't imagine that either, but she didn't say so. However, it did make her want to prolong this evening for as long as possible, and if that meant what she thought it meant, then so be it. She had to lose her virginity sooner or later, she reminded herself, and she'd rather it was with him than someone else.

Cupping his face in her hands, she opened her mouth against his and felt his teeth bite into the lower lip. But, 'I can't do this,' he said against her lips, and with a muffled oath he thrust himself up and away from her.

Helen was devastated. She'd thought he was as committed as she was, but it was obvious he was still in control of his feelings. With a little moan of anguish, she turned onto her side facing the back of the sofa, burying her suddenly tear-wet face in the cushions.

'Don't,' she heard him say in a tortured voice. 'Helen, don't make me despise myself, any more than I do already.'

'You don't despise yourself,' she muttered, her voice muffled against the soft fabric. 'You despise me.' She broke off with a sob. 'I should never have come here.'

'You're probably right,' Milos agreed harshly, but now his voice was much nearer, and when she rolled onto her back she found him hunkered down beside her. He put out his hand, his thumb smearing a tear from her wet cheek. '*Moro mou,* what am I going to do with you?'

Helen sniffed. 'What do you want to do with me?'

'Now that's an unnecessary question, and you know it,' he said unevenly. 'If I said I wanted to take you to bed, to take away all your clothes so I could look at you, you'd run a mile.'

'Why?'

'Oh, please—' Milos shook his head, his thumb moving to her mouth and running almost cruelly over her lips. 'We both know you've never done anything like this before.'

Helen's face burned. 'How do you know?'

For an answer, Milos moved his hand to the juncture of her legs, cupping her mound with a practised hand and causing her to buck a little jerkily beneath his touch. 'See,' he said softly. 'I don't need any more proof.'

'You—you startled me, that's all,' she protested, but Milos only gave her an old-fashioned look.

'Oh, right,' he said drily. 'I suggest you dry your eyes and I'll take you home.'

'I don't want to go home.'

He scowled. 'What you're doing is—dangerous.'

'Because you want me?'

'Get up, Helen.' Milos gnawed at his bottom lip. 'Don't make me have to do it for you.'

Her lips trembled a little, but she didn't move. If he wanted her to leave, he would have to make her. She wasn't going to make it easy for him.

'Helen!' he said grimly, speaking through his teeth.

'Milos!' she countered.

He swore then and, with some force, he thrust his arms beneath her and hauled her up into his arms. He got to his feet and for a heartstopping moment he held her there, cradled against his chest, their eyes, their mouths, only inches apart. Then, determinedly, he lowered her to the floor.

But it didn't work out as he'd intended. Her arms were around his neck and when he set her on her feet they stayed where they were. In fact, his action had only added to their intimacy, her limbs sliding silkily against his aroused body.

'*Theos*, Helen,' he said hoarsely, but she sensed it was no longer a protest. They'd both proved their points in different ways, and he gave a sigh of defeat. 'Yes, I want you,' he added as his arms closed about her. 'I just hope you won't regret this in the morning.'

CHAPTER TWELVE

RHEA drove them back to the vineyard in the late afternoon. Surprisingly, Melissa had fallen asleep after lunch and although Helen would have woken her, Rhea had persuaded her to change her mind.

'She's tired,' she said. 'She's had a strenuous morning. Let her rest.'

In the circumstances, Helen decided not to argue. And it was true, Melissa was probably worn out. But she suspected Rhea's motives for wanting them to stay had more to do with wanting to know about her brother's apparent interest in herself and what it might mean to his family.

Leaving her daughter drowsing in the shade of the terrace, Helen accepted Rhea's invitation to walk with her in the gardens. Despite the bare hillside that fell away below the villa, within its walls someone had created an oasis of colour. Terraces of exotic blooms and flowering shrubs hid a tumbling waterfall, and on the lowest level a stone bench was set beneath an arching pergola that was covered with purple bougainvillea.

'Shall we sit?' suggested Rhea, but it was hardly a question. She seated herself without waiting for her guest's acquiescence, and Helen had little choice but to join her.

'So,' Rhea continued, immediately getting to the point, 'how long have you known my brother?'

Despite her suspicions, Helen was taken aback. 'I—beg your pardon?'

Rhea arched a dark brow. 'I asked how long—'

'Yes, I know what you said.' Helen took a moment to gather herself. 'I—just wonder why you feel you have to ask such a question?'

'Oh…' Rhea was thoughtful. 'Put it down to sibling curiosity. I can't remember the last time Milos invited a woman to his home.'

'He didn't exactly invite me to his home.'

'Oh, he did.' Rhea was very sure of that. 'I was left in no doubt that he wanted to talk to you. Alone.'

Helen felt the heat rising up her face. 'Then why didn't he invite me himself?' she countered stiffly, and Rhea shrugged.

'Perhaps he didn't believe you'd accept his invitation.'

Helen tried to be dismissive. 'I can't believe that.'

'Can't you?' Rhea's eyes were almost as direct as her brother's, which was disconcerting in itself. 'Helen, I know my brother. I know him very well, actually. He was very definite about what he wanted me to do.'

'Well, I'm sorry if you feel he was using you to get to me—'

'I didn't say that.' Though they both knew she had. 'I don't want to offend you, Helen. I'd just like to know how the two of you met. That's not so difficult to understand, is it?'

'No.' Helen moistened her lips. 'But your brother's a—a very attractive man, Rhea. I imagine he meets lots of women in the course of his travels.'

'I imagine he does.' Rhea sighed. 'But Milos is not a—what is that word?—a womaniser, *okhi*? I think I can count on one hand the number of women he has introduced to me.'

Helen didn't have an answer for that, so instead she decided to be honest. Well, as honest as it was necessary to be, anyway. 'He—we—I met him— oh—' she mustn't be too definite '—perhaps a dozen years ago. In England.'

Rhea's eyes widened. '*Psemata?* Really?'

'Yes, really.' Helen tried to sound casual about it. 'My—er—my father had asked him to look me up.'

'*Katalava.* I see.' Rhea absorbed this with interest. 'I wonder why he didn't tell me that?'

'I don't suppose he considered it important.'

'But—you must have been very young at that time.'

'Not so young,' said Helen, hurriedly trying to calculate how old she'd have been twelve years ago. 'I—er—I was about twenty.'

'Ah.' Rhea's eyebrows lifted even further, and Helen realised that by exaggerating her age, she had inadvertently given Rhea a reason to think there might have been more than friendship between them.

'Anyway,' she said, hoping to divert her, 'I suppose you'd still have been in primary school then.'

'I guess.' But Rhea wasn't interested in her own past now. 'imagine,' she said reflectively. 'You and Milos have known one another since almost before Melissa was born. Were you married when you met? Of course, you must have been.'

This was getting more and more complicated and Helen strove desperately for a lifeline. 'You must love coming here,' she said, gesturing at the view. 'Who looks after the garden? Your mother?'

'Hardly.' Rhea giggled a little at that. 'If you ever meet my mother you'll understand how unlikely that scenario is. Athene is an ornament, not a worker. She considers giving my father five children was quite enough.'

Helen managed a polite smile and she was relieved when Rhea went on in a different vein. 'But, yes, I do love coming here. It's so much more appealing than the college apartment I share with a girlfriend in Athens.'

'Oh, but surely you could—'

Helen broke off and Rhea finished the sentence for her. 'Live at home?' she queried. 'Well, yes, I could. But I wanted to be independent. To prove I could— what do you say?—hack it, *ne*, with my fellow students? Unfortunately Papa was right. I would have been more comfortable living with them.'

'So you come here when you can?' Helen breathed a little more easily. 'I don't blame you. It's very beautiful.'

'You like it?' Rhea stared at her and Helen could almost see the cogs of her brain turning.

'Very much,' she said.

Rhea frowned. 'Melissa must just have been a baby when you met Milos,' she said, returning to her previous theme, and Helen suppressed a groan.

'I—suppose she must have been,' she said, hating the lie, but unable to do anything about it. She got determinedly to her feet. 'I really think we ought to be going now.'

Rhea squinted in the sunlight as she looked up at her. 'I've embarrassed you.'

'No.' Helen spoke sharply. 'Why—?'

'Talking about Milos,' broke in Rhea softly. 'I get the feeling there was more to your relationship than just a casual encounter.'

'You're wrong.' But Helen was breathing faster now and she knew the other girl had noticed.

'I'm not suggesting you had an affair,' Rhea continued lightly. 'After all, you were married, as you say. But I know how attractive my brother is. And he was obviously quite—intrigued—by you.'

'No.'

It was all Helen could think of, but Rhea wasn't to be put off. 'There is some history there, I know it,' she said. 'And if you will not tell me, then I will just have to ask Milos. *Then pirazi*, it doesn't matter. Shall we go and see if Melissa is awake?'

Conversely, Helen was loath to leave the subject now. She dreaded to think what Milos would say if Rhea asked him how they'd met. And if he gave her different dates, she was bound to be suspicious. Oh, what a tangled web she'd woven for herself.

But there was nothing she could do or say to change things now and she was grateful that Melissa's chatter meant there were no awkward silences on the journey home. The younger girl had awoken from her nap full of energy and eager to arrange another meeting with Rhea.

Helen wished there were some way she could discourage their association, but there wasn't. Not without alienating her daughter, anyway. She just wished she didn't have the feeling that Rhea might be using her friendship with Melissa to find out more about Melissa's mother.

It was a relief of sorts when Rhea dropped them at Aghios Petros and took her leave. Melissa insisted on going to see her off and Sam Campbell, who had offered the Greek girl a drink, which she had declined, now invited his daughter to join him as he checked on the grapes.

She realised it had just been an excuse for them to be alone together when he said abruptly, 'You didn't enjoy it, did you? Melissa obviously did, but you didn't.'

Helen sighed. 'Rhea and Melissa have more in common with each other,' she replied, forcing a light tone. Then, once again taking the defensive, 'Have you had a good day?'

'Is it Milos?' Her father was either astonishingly shrewd or Helen's face was pathetically easy to read. 'You've seen him today, haven't you?'

'How do you know that?'

Her father shrugged. 'Does it matter?'

Helen bit her lip. 'Well, only for a short while,' she admitted, not altogether truthfully. 'He left for Athens—'

'Not until this afternoon, surely,' remarked her father mildly. 'I spoke to him a couple of hours ago from the helicopter.' He paused. 'He told me he'd taken you to Vassilios. Did you like it?'

Did she like it? Helen knew an almost hysterical desire to laugh. 'I—thought it was an impressive house,' she said at last, wishing she could escape all these questions. She had thought that she'd be free of them once Rhea had left.

'Did Melissa go with you?'

'I—no.' Helen was obliged to be truthful. 'She

and Rhea went to the beach. I'd have liked to go with them.'

'But you didn't.'

'No.'

'Because Milos invited you to see his house?'

Because Milos *insisted* she see his house, Helen wanted to answer tersely. But all she said was, 'Yes,' hoping Sam would leave it at that.

Of course, he didn't. 'You dislike Milos, don't you?' he said, picking a handful of tiny green grapes from the vine and handing them to her to taste. 'I'm curious why. What happened between you two when he came to England? He must have done something to make you dislike him so much.'

'I don't dislike him.' Helen used the grapes as an excuse to turn away. 'Mmm, these are really delicious.'

'They're not sweet enough yet,' said her father drily. 'In another three months, they'll taste altogether different.' He hesitated. 'I'd like to think you and Melissa would visit us again for the harvest. I hope it's not my imagination, but I think Melissa has changed since she came here.'

At last, Helen could speak freely. 'Oh, she has,' she said eagerly. 'I think she needed a masculine influence in her life. Since Richard—well, since Richard died, she has become increasingly rebellious. Although I have to admit, she wasn't much different when he was alive.'

'She never talks about him, you know.'

'I know,' Helen sighed. 'That used to worry me, too.'

'Mmm.' Her father was thoughtful. 'She doesn't seem to have any problem in talking to Milos.'

'She hardly knows him.' Helen tried to sound dismissive.

'I wouldn't say that.' Sam was persistent. 'You should have heard her chatting to him the other evening when you were talking to Alex. I think she likes him. A lot. I just wish you felt the same.'

'Dad!'

'What?' He held up his hands in self defence. 'Milos is a good friend of mine, and Maya's. Is it so unreasonable that I'd like my daughter to show him some respect?'

'I do respect him,' said Helen shortly, glancing back towards the house. 'I'm sorry if you think I've been rude. That wasn't my intention.'

'I didn't say you'd been rude to him,' Sam corrected her mildly. 'But you must see how you react when I mention his name. You're immediately on the defensive.'

Helen shook her head. 'I haven't noticed it,' she muttered, but of course she had. 'Look, I'm feeling rather sticky. I need a shower. Would you mind if I—?'

'I think he's attracted to you,' Sam interrupted her, and Helen's jaw dropped.

'Don't be so ridiculous!'

'What's ridiculous about it?' Sam was unperturbed by her reactions. 'It was he who invited you to San Rocco, wasn't it? Not Rhea. Oh, yes, he told me all about it. He said he thought you might refuse the invitation if you'd known it had come from him. And you would have, wouldn't you? You've just proved it.'

Helen didn't know what to say. 'I—all right, yes. I would have refused. I don't think it's a good idea to let Melissa think that we have anything in common with people like them.'

'Milos and Rhea, you mean?'

'Who else?'

'But why?' Sam's tone gentled. 'What's your objection? Are you afraid of what people will say if you admit to being interested in another man less than a year after your husband was killed?'

'No!'

'So what is it?'

'Oh, Dad!' For the second time in as many minutes, Helen used the familiar form of address without even thinking about it. 'Men like Milos Stephanides do not get involved with—with women like me.'

'How right you are,' declared a contemptuous voice from behind them, and Helen turned to find Maya striding towards them along the row of vines. The woman made some other vituperative comment in her own language and then, when her husband remonstrated with her, she added irritably, '*Kalia*, you are filling the girl's head with nonsense, Samuel. How many times must Milos tell you he is not interested in marrying again. Nor in having meaningless affairs. Is that not good enough for you?'

Helen made her escape then, telling herself she was glad Maya had interrupted them. Despite her protestations, the temptation to listen to what her father had had to say had been appealing. She didn't believe it; would never believe Milos had had anything more than a fleeting flirtation in mind when he'd first invited her to have a drink with him. But it was flattering nonetheless.

Of course, if her father knew the truth he'd have an entirely different outlook on the situation. And when he'd first mentioned Richard, and Melissa's liking for Milos, she'd been half afraid he'd guessed who the child's father was.

But she was worrying unnecessarily. The only way Sam could find out about that was if he learned it from her, and she couldn't tell him. Not because she didn't want to, she acknowledged painfully. But because he would insist on telling Milos, and her whole relationship with her daughter would be put in jeopardy.

Was she being selfish? In her heart of hearts, she rather thought she was. But how could she risk losing the only child she was ever likely to have?

She wondered if she'd have surrendered herself to Milos so willingly if she'd known what a shattering effect he was going to have on her life. The answer was obvious, but at that time it hadn't seemed such a big deal. Seduced by Milos's love-making—and the champagne—she'd given herself to him with a joyful abandon she could hardly conceive of now. When had she acquired such a belief that what she was doing was right? She seemed to have forgotten everything she'd ever been taught about sex and its aftermath. She'd been warned often enough that condoms were not always foolproof.

At the time of course, she hadn't been thinking of things like that, and now, as she stood in the shower, letting the cool water cascade over her hot skin, she had to admit that she had been as much to blame for what had happened as Milos. Oh, she might have had less reason to worry about the future—she hadn't been married, for one thing— but she had done everything she could to break down his control, to make him as much at the mercy of his feelings as she was.

And she'd succeeded. She'd known the moment he'd said in that hoarse, sexy voice, 'Yes, I want you,' that she'd got her way.

She shivered in the cool spray, remembering the tormented look in his eyes when he'd drawn back to cradle her hot face between his palms. Then, as if seeing a reflection of his own needs in her eyes, he'd taken her hand and led her into his bedroom.

A bedroom that had been every bit as glamorous as she'd imagined, Helen recalled tensely. There'd been long velour curtains at the windows that matched the deep gold piled carpet on the floor. The bed had already been turned down for the night, the coverlet folded neatly at its foot. There'd been soft pillows, edged with lace, and fine cotton sheets that had been cool against her hot skin.

Her shirt had already been unbuttoned and Milos had paused to tug on the ties at her waist before slipping it off her shoulders. She'd been trembling, she remembered, when he'd unfastened her jeans, but she couldn't recall any moment when she'd wanted to draw back.

'You, too,' she said, reaching for the buttons on his shirt, and Milos humoured her by shrugging off his shirt before slipping his hands behind her to loosen her bra.

It joined her shirt on the floor and then Milos took her breasts into his hands, his thumbs rubbing abrasively over her sensitive nipples.

'Is that good?' he asked, hearing her sudden intake of breath, and Helen had swayed eagerly against him.

'Some,' she whispered, sliding her arms around his waist, hooking her fingers into the waistband of his trousers. Her breasts were now crushed against his chest, the hair that grew there both tickling and arousing her. 'But I want more.'

With hands that were only slightly less unsteady than her own, Helen remembered Milos feeling between them to unbuckle his trousers, before taking one of her hands and pressing it against the impressive bulge swelling beneath his silk boxers. She remembered how big and powerful his erection had felt and even now she felt her body grow slick with the same anticipation she'd felt then.

Afterwards, he knelt in front of her, drawing her jeans down her legs, exposing the bikini pants that were all she was wearing underneath. He lifted each leg almost tenderly, disposing of the jeans with gentle expertise.

When he straightened again, it was to thrust his own trousers down his thighs, kicking them off almost carelessly. Helen recalled that that was when she'd become aware of her own body and of the fact that she was standing before him almost naked.

He had—still did, for that matter—a lean, powerful body. Strong, athletic limbs, a broad muscled chest, flat stomach. And he was brown; all over, she mused enviously. A natural tan that owed nothing to artificial means.

His kiss, when it came, was warm and searching. It tingled on lips that were still swollen from his previous assault. Helen had to clutch helplessly at his shoulders as the kiss deepened, her legs turning to jelly beneath her.

She thought he half nudged, half carried her to the bed, murmuring to her in his own language, words that even now could cause a shiver of excitement to feather her spine. Her skin felt so tender, she remembered, so sensitised; as if he'd somehow removed a layer to expose the vulnerable flesh beneath. But she unbearably stimulated, too, and she almost welcomed the cool brush of the sheets against her bare back.

Helen stepped out of the shower now, aware that she was arousing herself again by even thinking about the events of that evening. There'd been something so extraordinarily decadent about being in bed so early in the evening, even if her reasons for being there had had little to do with sleep.

When Milos had stretched his length beside her, she'd turned to him with all the resistance of the moth to the flame. He'd been naked, she'd discovered, and she hadn't been able to prevent herself from staring at him. It was the first time she'd actually seen a nude male outside movies, and, far from feeling apprehensive, she'd been fascinated.

'You're embarrassing me,' Milos said huskily, burying his face between her breasts. But Helen had the feeling now that it would have taken a lot more than her innocent appraisal to embarrass him.

'Am I?' she recalled saying, with a pathetic attempt at coyness, but Milos's hands were sliding down her body and a quivering knot twisted in her belly.

She did remember being a little apprehensive when his fingers slid over her stomach and beneath the elastic waist of her briefs. He probed the tight curls at the apex of her legs, and Helen had to suck back the convulsive sob that surged into her throat.

Her instincts were urging her to open her legs and let him have his way with her, but her conscience was less certain and instead she pressed her legs together.

'Relax,' Milos breathed into her ear, catching the soft lobe between his teeth and biting on it almost painfully. 'Just relax. You know you want to.'

And, amazingly, she did. When Milos eased her briefs down her legs, she arched her back to make it easy for him. Then somehow her legs were parted, and she could feel her wetness on his hands. On the sure and certain fingers he pressed into her.

His thumb had other work to do, rotating the sensitive nub of her womanhood with such effortless expertise that she climaxed almost immediately. Of course, she didn't know what was happening to her. She was comparatively naïve, after all, despite all Richard's efforts in that regard.

She remembered she was laughing and crying with wonder when he parted her legs again and positioned himself above her. So bemused was she that she hardly felt any pain when he pushed into her. And, although there was a momentary hesitation on his part when he encountered the unmistakable proof of her virginity, he was much too aroused to draw back. Besides, she didn't want him to. She wanted to feel him inside her. And, even though initially it wasn't the most comfortable position in the world, as her body accommodated itself to his size, the exquisite excitement started to build again.

Helen trembled now, shocked by the awareness of how sharp the memories were. She would have thought that what had happened after would have soured the feelings Milos had stirred inside her, but it wasn't true. They were still as acute and devastating as ever, causing not just frustration but a painful need inside her.

She wondered how old Milos had been at that time. Twenty-two, perhaps? Twenty-three? Certainly no more than twenty-four. Yet he had had a skill and sensitivity that had seemed as natural as breathing to him. He'd given her the most marvellous experience of her life—and the most shattering. With hindsight, it was difficult to decide which was the most important.

At the time, she'd been sure she knew. Milos had made love to her with a warmth and passion that she'd never experienced either before or since. With his innate sensuality, he'd ensured that she'd achieved an equal satisfaction, and when his own climax had left him shuddering in her arms she'd been happy to share his pleasure, too.

Of course, Eleni's phone call had proved to be equally devastating. Or perhaps destructive was a more appropriate word. Her call had come as Helen had been drowsing against the pillows, her body and mind still sated by the delicious aftermath of Milos's passion, and to begin with she hadn't been able to make any sense of what the other woman was saying.

She'd soon understood, however, and then it had been a race to get herself dressed and out of there before Milos came out of the bathroom and she had to confront him with his lies. She hadn't felt equipped to deal with him, or with anything so earth-shattering that night. But she had been absurdly grateful that Milos had collected her parka from the attendant before they'd gone upstairs. In her haste to get away before he could demand an explanation, the parka had hid a multitude of sins.

She remembered taking the lift down to the lobby, fretting every inch of the way, and flying out of the hotel as if Lucifer himself were at her heels. She'd refused the doorman's offer to get her a taxi. She hadn't dared wait for that to materialise. Instead, she'd run madly for over half a mile to the nearest depot from where she could get a bus home.

Thankfully, her mother had noticed nothing amiss. Helen had had time on the bus to finish dressing herself, fastening her buttons and running a hasty comb through her long hair. Besides, she'd been home before ten-thirty, as her mother had requested, and perhaps Sheila hadn't wanted to push her luck.

Whatever, the next few days had been uneasy ones for Helen. Every time the phone had rung, she'd rushed to answer it, desperate that her mother shouldn't find out what a stupid fool she'd been. She hadn't known whether she could trust Milos not to tell her mother that he'd seen her, and, although she'd been fairly sure he wouldn't tell Sheila what had happened, she'd wanted nothing more to do with him.

He'd soon got the message, she remembered. Humiliatingly soon, actually. Oh, he insisted now that he'd had to get back to Athens because he'd had business to attend to, but how convenient was that?

Her lips tightened. Would she have been so quick to reject his advances if she'd known she was carrying his baby? she wondered. Probably. How could she have confided in him, believing he already had a wife waiting for him back in Greece? That would have been even more humiliating, and at no time had she seriously considered it.

Instead, she'd confessed what she'd done to Richard Shaw. She'd let him think she'd gone to a party, given by one of her mother's friends, and that she'd had too much to drink. Which wasn't that far from the truth, she reflected drily. Only Milos Stephanides had been no friend of her mother's.

Still, Richard had believed her, that was the important thing, and when he'd offered to marry her she'd taken the coward's way out. The only condition Richard had imposed was that she let everybody—and that included her mother—believe the baby was his. And that had seemed a reasonable request.

Of course, her mother had left her in no doubt that she was disappointed in her for getting pregnant. She'd let her down and, in Sheila's opinion, marrying Richard was the only way she could save the family from any more disgrace.

Nevertheless, at seventeen, she knew she had been too young to take such a momentous step. The more sensible thing would have been to wait until after the baby was born before making any life-altering decisions. But that she hadn't been able to do. Not without support, and her mother had left her in no doubt as to her opinion. And right then, it had seemed the only solution.

Helen sighed, shedding the towel in favour of

the bra and pants she'd brought into the bathroom with her. But before she put her underwear on, she stood for a moment staring at her reflection in the long mirrors.

A woman of middle years looked back at her, no longer the innocent she'd been when she and Milos had first met. Yet she hadn't changed that much, she thought critically. Not physically, anyway. She was still fairly slim, and if her breasts were heavier these days, that was because she'd insisted on feeding her baby herself for the first three months of Melissa's life. Her hips were rounder, too, and she could see the faint traces of stretch marks on her abdomen. She was no raving beauty, that was certain. So why had Milos wanted to see her again? Why had he kissed her? Weren't there enough Greek women to satisfy his every need?

CHAPTER THIRTEEN

IT WAS another four days before Milos was able to get back to Santoros.

The conference had been a huge success, with many oil-producing countries signing up to a pollution-reducing treaty. But, because of that, all the delegates were expected to stay for the duration of the event, which included attending the final evening's celebrations, when the wives of many of those present joined their husbands for a formal dinner of congratulations and speech-making.

Milos would definitely have preferred not to attend the dinner. He had no desire to invite a companion to join him for the evening. But as the company's representative he couldn't get out of it, and he spent the evening dodging the matchmaking efforts of his fellow delegates.

It was a relief to get on board his helicopter the following morning and know that he had no further business commitments for the next few days. He had his laptop with him, of course, and he had no doubt that there would be certain communications he would have to make. But, effectively, he had a few days of freedom and he meant to make the most of them.

With Helen.

As the pilot took off, the helicopter's rotors dipping for a moment as it turned towards the island, Milos felt a twinge of apprehension that had nothing to do with his mode of transport. It was the anxiety he was feeling at the thought of seeing Helen again, of gauging for himself whether what had happened the day he left had meant anything to her. And if it hadn't, what he was going to do about it.

Which was probably insane, given the circumstances of their relationship. How could he have feelings for a woman who had consistently lied since she'd arrived on the island? And why? What was she trying to protect? Her guilt? Or her husband's memory?

That was an aspect he hadn't considered before, and he didn't like it. Any time during the past few days when his mind hadn't been fully engaged, his thoughts had turned constantly to Helen. And to contemplate the possibility that she still loved her dead husband tore him apart.

He'd thought about Melissa, too, of course, but in his mind her future was so tied up with her mother's that he didn't worry about her in quite the same way. He wanted to be part of her life from now on, naturally he did, and he couldn't deny he'd considered the part she might play in persuading Helen to do what he wanted. But he was not a malicious man and he knew that forcing Helen into a situation that was abhorrent to her by threatening to take her daughter was not what he wanted.

So what did he want? he wondered as the helicopter swept out across the blue waters of the Aegean. He wanted—no, *needed*—to see Helen again. That was his first objective. In truth, he couldn't wait to see her, to talk to her, to *touch* her, although that might be a harder call. It was all very well asking himself if he could forgive her. What if she couldn't forgive him?

The hardest thing he'd faced during the past four days had been resisting the desire to call Rhea. He was fairly sure that she and Melissa would have spent some time together, and the urge to hear firsthand what Helen had been doing while he was away had been a constant temptation.

But he'd withstood it, and now he was glad

he had. These few days apart had focussed his mind—and, hopefully, hers, too. Could they possibly make a fresh start? Was he naïve in thinking that this time something good might come of it?

His pilot landed at Vassilios just before twelve o'clock, and as usual Stelios was there to greet him. 'Welcome back, *kirieh*,' he said, meeting him at the landing pad that was situated at the back of the villa. 'It has been a good trip, yes?'

'Very good,' agreed Milos, giving the answer he knew was expected. 'Is everything okay? Is Andrea keeping well? Would you tell her I expect to be dining at home this evening?'

'Alone, *kirieh*?' Stelios asked politely as they walked up to the terrace. And Milos hoped he wasn't tempting fate by telling the man that he expected a guest to join him.

'I'll confirm the time we want to eat later this afternoon,' he went on. 'Right now, I want to drive over to San Rocco and see my sister.'

'*Kiria* Rhea, *kirieh*?'

Milos's lips compressed. He really didn't have the patience to discuss his plans right now. 'Who else?' he replied tersely. 'Now, if you'll excuse me, Stelios—'

'*Kiria* Rhea isn't at the villa at San Rocco,

kirieh.' Stelios interrupted him mildly as Milos started towards the house. 'I believe she's staying at Aghios Petros, with *Thespinis* Melissa.'

What?

Milos stared at the man irritably, but it wasn't Stelios's fault that his plans had just been baulked. 'I didn't know that,' he said, revising rapidly. He would probably have to wait to talk to Rhea until the following day.

'I believe she tried to call you yesterday evening,' Stelios continued. 'But you were not answering your phone.'

'No.' Miles swore under his breath. He'd turned his cell phone off before going to the farewell dinner. 'I just wish she'd told me before she decided to leave the villa.'

'I think it was a —how is it?— a spur-of-the-moment decision, *kirieh*. You were out of reach. I suppose she thought it was for the best.'

'For the best?' Milos blinked. 'What happened? Did she burn the villa down or something?'

'No, *kirieh*.' There was no humour in Stelios's expression. 'It is my understanding that it was considered to be the best solution for all concerned.'

Milos was beginning to get a bad feeling about

all of this. 'The best solution?' he exclaimed, echoing Stelios's words again, but needing some explanation. 'Did—?' He hated to ask it. 'Did *Kiria* Shaw invite her to stay?'

'*Kiria* Shaw?' Now it was Stelios's turn to look confused. Then his face cleared. 'Oh, you mean *Kirieh* Campbell's daughter,' he said.

'That's right.' Milos was trying not to get impatient with the old man, but it wasn't easy. 'The young woman I brought to Vassilios four days ago.'

'Ah.' Stelios nodded. 'I thought you knew. *Kiria* Shaw has gone back to England.'

To say Milos was stunned would have been an understatement. He felt as if the bottom had just dropped out of his world. 'Did you say *Kiria* Shaw has gone back to England?' he demanded hoarsely. He tried to think, raking back his hair with an unsteady hand. 'When did she leave?'

'I believe she left the day after you did,' replied Stelios, unaware of his employer's agitation. 'That would be Friday, wouldn't it? That's right, you left on Thursday afternoon.'

'I know when I left,' said Milos grimly. 'I just don't understand why she left, dammit.' He shook his head. 'What the hell is going on?'

Stelios stiffened. It was as if he'd just realised that he was bearing the brunt of Milos's frustration and he didn't like it. 'I have no idea, *kirieh*,' he said, even though Milos was sure he did. 'Shall I tell Andrea you'll be wanting lunch, after all?'

Milos sighed. 'No!' He scowled, realising the old man was offended. 'Stelios, I know you know much more than you're saying. I'm sorry if I spoke harshly, but—well, this isn't what I expected when I came back.'

'I don't suppose it was what *Kiria* Shaw expected either, *kirieh*,' retorted Stelios primly. 'Now, about lunch—'

Milos was tempted to say, To hell with lunch, but he knew getting angry with Stelios wasn't going to work. 'Come on,' he said wheedlingly. 'We're friends, aren't we? I would appreciate it if you'd tell me what's going on.'

Stelios's shoulders hunched, half in resentment, half in resignation. Then, reproachfully, he said, 'I believe *Kiria* Shaw received some bad news.'

Milos's scowl deepened. 'What kind of bad news?' A thought occurred to him. 'Had it anything to do with her mother?'

'You said you didn't know, *kirieh*,' complained

Stelios reproachfully. 'If you only wanted confirmation, you should have said.'

Milos bit his tongue to prevent his anger from spilling over. He had to remember this wasn't Stelios's fault, even if he did have the urge to seize him by the throat and choke an explanation out of him. 'I don't,' he said between his teeth, congratulating himself on his tolerance. 'But as she's *Kiria* Shaw's closest relative, it was an educated guess.'

Stelios pressed his lips together for a moment before speaking. Then, 'It's only hearsay,' he said. 'You do understand that, don't you, *kirieh*?'

'Okay.' Milos nodded. 'So what have you heard?'

'I understand *Kiria* Shaw's mother has been injured in a car accident, *kirieh*,' the old man admitted, half grudgingly, and Milos's spirits plummeted at his words.

'Badly injured?' he demanded, but Stelios decided he had said enough.

'I suggest you ask *Kirieh* Campbell,' he said, picking up the suit carrier Milos had put down as they spoke. 'I'll take this to your room, *kirieh*. It will give you time to decide whether you want lunch or not.'

Despite the fact that he would have preferred to speak to Rhea alone, Milos drove over to the vineyard that afternoon.

It occurred to him that his decision might appear unnecessarily arbitrary, but he consoled himself with the thought that Rhea was his sister and it was natural to want to assure himself of her well-being. The fact that in other circumstances he might not have behaved so considerately was something he chose not to dwell on.

In the event, it was Maya who came out to greet him on his arrival. 'Darling,' she exclaimed, speaking in their own language as she always did when they were alone. 'I didn't realise you were back.'

'I got back this morning,' said Milos evenly, wondering how he could broach the reason for his visit. But before he could say anything else, Maya spoke again.

'And was the conference a success?' she asked, taking possession of his arm to lead him into the villa. 'We've heard certain details about it on the television news, but that's not the same as being there—'

'Maya!'

'—is it?' she continued, as if he hadn't spoken. 'I understand the speech you gave offered a compelling argument in favour of reducing oil pollution. Didn't the Prime Minister himself compliment you on it? I tell you, we were so proud—'

'Maya!' This time Milos made sure she heard him. Releasing himself from her clinging fingers, he put a tangible distance between them before saying, 'I understand Rhea's staying with you at the moment.'

Maya's lips tightened. 'Oh. Oh, yes, she is.' She paused. 'It was Sam's idea, not mine.'

'I see.' Milos wondered what he had to say to make her realise he wanted to know what was going on. 'Why was that?'

Maya gave him a swift sideways look. 'You know Helen's gone back to England, don't you?'

'I—heard something about it,' Milos conceded, unable to deny it. 'Her mother's had an accident, I believe.'

'Sheila. Yes.' Maya's expression was grim. 'Do you know, Sam wanted to go with Helen.'

'And did he?'

'No.' Maya squared her shoulders defiantly. 'I told him, the fact that Sheila's had an accident is nothing to do with you. Happily, he saw reason.'

'Perhaps he only wanted to keep his daughter

company,' offered Milos tightly. 'Was she very upset?'

Maya shrugged. 'She got a shock, I suppose. Personally, I'm not at all convinced the woman didn't cause the accident on purpose. She never wanted Helen to come out here in the first place.'

Milos had guessed that for himself, but he thought Maya was being unnecessarily harsh. 'Surely no one would deliberately injure themselves, whatever the reason?' he remarked mildly. Then, taking a deep breath, 'So—when is Helen coming back?'

'I don't know.' Maya made a dismissive gesture. 'Perhaps she won't come back. I suppose it depends on how badly hurt her mother is and whether she'll need constant attention when she comes home from hospital.'

'She's in hospital?' Milos was dismayed.

'Oh, yes.' Maya nodded. 'It was the hospital who contacted us. Naturally Helen had to leave right away.'

Milos suppressed an inward groan. This was worse, much worse, than he'd expected. 'But Melissa stayed here.'

'Yes. Much good it's done her.' Maya was impatient. 'She's been moping about for days, ever since her mother left, actually. I'd have thought she'd be grateful to extend her holiday, but I was wrong.'

'So that's why Sam asked Rhea to stay?'

'I suppose.' Maya's nostrils flared. 'Well, never mind that now. Come and have a drink. You can tell me all about the conference—'

'Milos!' Melissa's excited voice interrupted them and for once he was inordinately grateful. 'When did you get here? Oh, I'm so glad you're back.'

The girl came charging across the entrance hall towards them and he thought for a moment that she was going to fling herself into his arms. But she stopped short of total abandon, halting a couple of feet from him and gazing at him with obvious relief.

'Hello, Melissa,' he said gently, thinking how different she looked now from the petulant teenager he'd met from the ferry. Her glossy dark hair was now free of the garish artificial colour she'd flaunted so proudly, and her face was clean of any cosmetics. She looked tanned and healthy, and so like Rhea he couldn't believe no one else had noticed.

She smiled at him a little tremulously, and he

realised she wasn't as confident as she appeared. 'Mum's not here.'

'I know.'

'You know about Gran's accident?'

'Of course, he knows,' exclaimed Maya, not at all pleased to have their conversation interrupted. She glanced past the girl to the terrace from where she'd appeared. 'Where's Rhea? Does she know her brother's here?'

'Rhea's in her room,' said Melissa, which wasn't exactly an answer. Then she took a step nearer to Milos. 'Have you come to take us to Vassilios?'

'Of course he hasn't come to take you to Vassilios,' retorted Maya shortly. 'As a matter of fact, we were in the middle of a conversation, Melissa. Why don't you go and find Rhea and tell her—?'

'There's no need for that.' Before he'd actually given any thought to what he was about to do, Milos reached out and took the girl's hand. 'You're looking good,' he said, pleased when her eyes brightened considerably. 'Is that a new outfit?'

'Rhea bought it for me,' she answered, glancing down at the cropped top and miniskirt that were liberally splashed in shades of red and orange. 'Do you really like it? It's not what I usually go for.'

'I'd noticed,' said Milos drily, but his lips

twitched with amusement. He hadn't realised how much he'd wanted to see his daughter again, too. 'So—would you like to come back to Vassilios with me?'

Melissa nodded eagerly. 'Rhea, too?'

'Of course,' said Milos, realising anything else would look very suspicious. They'd be thinking he had designs on his own daughter, he thought impatiently. When all he really wanted to do was talk to her about her mother.

'That'd be great,' said Melissa, pulling her hand away from his and heading for the stairs. 'I'll go and tell Rhea.'

'I suppose you realise you're only pandering to that child's wishes,' Maya muttered as Melissa bounded off to find the other girl, and Milos sighed.

'She's lonely,' he said, not wanting to get into an argument with his cousin.

'Aren't we all?' retorted Maya resentfully. 'Since that woman and her daughter came here, Sam's had no time for Alex and me at all.'

'That's not true, Maya.' Unknown to them, Sam had come in the outer door as she was speaking and now he gave his wife a reproachful look. 'But Helen and I have got so many years to make up.

Surely you don't begrudge her a few weeks of my time?'

Maya looked embarrassed now. 'No,' she mumbled, showing she wasn't entirely without feelings. 'I know you mean well, Sam. But how long do you expect them to stay? I understood they were coming for a few days, two weeks at the most. Instead of which, you're talking as if you'd like them to live here.'

'I would.' Sam was honest enough to admit it. 'But that's not going to happen, is it? Her mother's never going to agree to that. So I'm making the most of what I have.'

Milos envied Sam his uncomplicated optimism. He was only just beginning to realise exactly what he'd lost. He should have spoken, he chided himself, before he'd left for Athens. If he hadn't been so absorbed in his own needs, his own desires, he'd have told Helen he wanted her and their daughter.

An hour later, he got his chance to speak to Rhea. With Melissa splashing about in the pool at Vassilios they were able to talk without being overheard.

'So what exactly happened?' he asked, referring to Sheila Campbell's accident. 'Do you know?'

'Well, according to her father, Helen's mother was reversing out of her drive at the time. She was apparently hit by a van coming along the road. It caught her on the side and she was crushed against the steering wheel.'

Milos winced. '*Theos*, it was serious then?'

'Why, yes.' Rhea glanced at him. 'Did you think it wasn't?'

'Oh...' Milos shook his head. 'It was just something Maya said. I got the impression from her that—'

'She thought it was a put-up job,' Rhea finished for him drily. 'Yes, I've heard that, too, but it's not true.'

Milos hesitated. 'So—has Sam heard from her since she got back to England?'

'Just once,' said Rhea, frowning as she spread sun cream liberally over her arms. 'She rang her father after she'd been to the hospital for the first time. She said that no one could tell her how long her mother was likely to stay there.'

Milos closed his eyes for a moment and then opened them again to find Rhea watching him closely. 'You're sorry she's not here,' she said, and it wasn't a question. 'Why do I get the feeling that there's something you're not telling me?'

'I can't imagine.' But Milos's eyes turned towards the pool as he spoke, the memory of the events of four days ago bringing a tightening to his jaw. 'However, I might suggest you and Melissa stay here until her mother returns. There's more room, for one thing, and you can see how much Melissa loves the water.'

Rhea gave him an ironic look. 'Like that's going to happen,' she said, and Milos thought with a pang that as much as his sister was influencing Melissa, Melissa was influencing her, too. 'Her grandfather's never going to agree to it,' she continued. 'However Maya feels about it, he's determined to maintain a presence in their lives from now on.'

'I'm not disputing that.'

But Milos's tone betrayed his irritation and Rhea cast him a considering stare. 'Are you in love with Helen?' she demanded. 'If you are, don't you think I should know about it? I am your sister, after all. Particularly as it's apparently been going on for several years.'

Milos's gaze swung back to her. 'I'm sure Helen didn't tell you that.'

'No.' Rhea sighed. 'But I got her to admit you'd first met years ago.'

Milos frowned. 'So what are you saying?'

Rhea flushed now. 'Well, only that you didn't mention it when you introduced us. Is it a secret? Is it because she was married at the time?'

Milos was appalled. Trying to calm his racing pulse, he said, 'What exactly did she tell you?'

Rhea shrugged. 'Well, she admitted she was married when you got to know one another.' Her eyes narrowed teasingly. 'You dark horse, Milos. I do believe you two had an affair.'

Milos shook his head. 'There was no affair.'

'But something was going on. Admit it.' Rhea stared at him with knowing eyes. 'I'm not stupid, Milos. Nor am I a little girl any more. When she admitted you two had met when you went to England, it was a simple matter to put two and two together.'

'And make three,' said Milos shortly. 'Forget it, Rhea. You've got it all wrong.'

'How? And why did you say three?' She frowned. 'Don't you mean five?'

'No, I mean three,' said Milos harshly. '*Theos*, Rhea, I don't know what Helen's told you, but she wasn't married when we met. She wasn't even pregnant, if you understand what I'm saying.'

* * *

Much later that evening, Milos sat alone on the terrace, drinking his way through a bottle of his father's Scotch. Aristotle always demanded single malt whisky when he came to visit, and Milos usually kept several bottles on the premises.

Tonight, however, he felt in need of something stronger than his usual glass of ouzo. He was in a foul mood, brought on by the knowledge that he'd unintentionally bared his soul to Rhea. He hadn't intended to tell her about Melissa, but somehow he hadn't been able to prevent himself. The need to defend both his and Helen's reputations overcoming any latent doubts he might have had.

And his sister had been marvellously supportive, even though she'd admitted she'd not noticed the resemblance between her and Melissa herself. Which hadn't exactly reassured him, torn as he was by his own doubts in the matter. What if he had made a mistake? What if Melissa was Richard Shaw's daughter, after all?

The only advantage he'd gained, if it was an advantage, was that Rhea had persuaded Sam to let the two girls spend the night at Vassilios. She had made the excuse of wanting to talk to Milos about her studies, and Sam had agreed that Melissa might benefit from a change of scene, too.

The two girls were both in bed, now, his house-keeper enjoying the novelty of having guests in the house for a change. Andrea had children and grandchildren of her own, and she was always delighted when one of Milos's siblings stayed over.

Milos poured himself another drink and glanced at his watch. In the light from the lanterns that were hung across the terrace, he could see it was after midnight. Time he was in bed, he thought, though he wasn't truly tired. He was weary, of course, after the events of the last few days, but he suspected his mind was too active to rest.

'Milos.'

He hadn't heard the sound of footsteps behind him. Not unnaturally, as Melissa was barefoot. Wearing only a skimpy pair of Rhea's pyjamas, she was hovering near the entrance to the villa and he wondered how long she had been standing there watching him.

'Hey,' he said, putting his ill humour aside and getting up from the lounge chair where he had been sitting. 'What are you doing out of bed?'

'I couldn't sleep,' said Melissa, taking a tentative step forward. 'Can I come and sit with you for a while?'

Milos refrained from saying he'd just been about

to retire himself. Instead, he gestured towards the chair beside him and waited until she was seated before offering her some juice. 'I won't offer you cola. That's not good for sleeping,' he said. 'But there are cans of orange juice in the cooler over there, if you want one.'

'I'm fine.' Melissa eased back on her chair stretching her bare legs out in front of her. 'Hmm, this is nice. I thought there'd be lots of insects and stuff.'

'Give it time,' said Milos drily, resuming his seat. 'So—why couldn't you sleep? Are you worrying about your grandmother?'

'I guess.' Melissa hunched her shoulders. 'Do you think she'll be all right?'

Milos didn't want to give her any false hopes, but he couldn't destroy them either. 'I'm sure she will,' he said, remembering it was less than a year since she'd had to deal with the death of the man she'd always believed to be her father. And in similar circumstances. 'Doctors can do wonders these days.'

'You think?' Melissa sniffed. 'I hope you're right.' She hesitated and then continued, 'She loves me, you see. Gran, I mean. And apart from her and Mum, there is nobody else.'

Milos's heart went out to her. 'I'm sure that's not true,' he said, wishing his own hands weren't tied in this way. 'There are lots of people who care about you. What about your grandfather?'

'Sam?' Melissa considered for a moment, but then she shook her head. 'No, there's just Mum and Gran,' she said, with a daunting conviction. 'I hate accidents, don't you? There's no warning or anything. Just—just a telephone call from the hospital.'

Milos sighed, realising he would have to bite the bullet. 'I suppose it's hard on you,' he said gently. 'After what happened to—to your father.'

'You mean Richard.' Melissa's head sunk lower into her shoulders as she spoke. 'Richard Shaw wasn't my father,' she added, barely audibly. 'He told me so at least two years before he died.'

CHAPTER FOURTEEN

IT WAS after ten o'clock when Helen arrived home. Although visiting hours at the hospital had ended some time ago, Helen had stopped off to buy some groceries they'd need when her mother came home.

The nurse in charge of her mother's case had been optimistic that Sheila Campbell might be able to return home in the next couple of days. The wound to her head was healing nicely, and although she still had a severe headache, a broken arm, and various cuts and bruises, none of them was life threatening.

Which hadn't seemed the case when Helen had first seen her. Sheila had been unconscious when she'd been brought to the hospital, and there'd been talk of skull fractures and possible coma. Her head wound had bled profusely, though Helen had been assured that this wasn't unusual. Nevertheless, her mother had certainly looked as bad as Helen's imagination had painted her.

During the past few days, however, the situation had changed considerably. As soon as Sheila had regained consciousness, it had become obvious her injuries weren't life-threatening as had originally been feared. In no time at all, she'd been ordering the nurses about, demanding the kind of treatment reserved for the more serious cases. She'd actually been outraged when they'd moved her out of the Intensive Care Unit, and installed her in the main ward.

This evening, Helen had been advised to prepare for her mother's discharge from the hospital. As soon as the specialist who'd been treating her was satisfied she was in no danger, she could go. The nurse had also warned Helen that Sheila would need a few days to get used to looking after herself, and that if Helen had a job she should arrange for a week's leave of absence to help her mother out.

Which meant Helen would not be able to return to Santoros. She should be grateful for that, she thought. Things between her and Milos had been getting too intense. Sitting beside her mother's bed while Sheila slept, she'd had plenty of time to worry about the future. Despite the fact that she wanted to spend more time with her father, it was probably wiser not to make promises she couldn't keep.

As she fumbled in her bag for her key she sensed someone behind her. Chiding herself for not getting her key out in the taxi she'd taken from the supermarket, she swung round, recklessly prepared to use her shopping as a weapon if she had to.

She dropped the plastic carrier a moment later. With cartons of butter and tins of soup spilling all over the garden path, she looked up into Milos's face and burst immediately into tears.

Milos didn't attempt to comfort her. Instead, he found her key and opened the door so that she could step inside. Then he set about gathering her scattered groceries together, filling the bag she'd dropped from nerveless fingers just a couple of minutes ago.

Dragging a tissue from her pocket, Helen dashed her tears away, humiliated that he of all people should see her like this. But it had all been too much: the shock of her mother's accident and the aftermath, and now Milos's appearance. She supposed she was desperately in need of someone to comfort her. But she doubted she'd get any comfort from him.

What was he doing here?

Switching on the light, she stumbled down the hall into the kitchen. She purposely avoided looking at her reflection in the unlit windows behind her, knowing she was definitely not looking her best. But she had spent the last few days running back and forward from the hospital. She'd had little time to think about her appearance, little time to do anything except live from day to day.

She heard the front door close and footsteps coming down the hall. Making a determined effort to school her features, she turned on the kitchen light and swung to face him. 'Thanks,' she said as he set the carrier on the top of one of the units. 'But that was a stupid thing to do.'

'Would it have been any less stupid if I'd spoken to you?' he asked, and Helen gave her shoulders a careless shrug.

'Probably not,' she agreed tersely. 'A phone call would have been more reasonable.' She squared her shoulders and faced him. 'What are you doing coming here at this time of night?'

Milos sighed. 'It wouldn't have been this time of night, as you put it, if you'd got home at the expected hour,' he said mildly. 'How was I to know you'd go shopping so late?'

'I was at the hospital till eight o'clock,' Helen said defensively. Her lips persisted in quivering as she spoke, and she pressed them together for a moment in an effort to calm herself. 'You—haven't been there, have you?' she added anxiously, and Milos gave her an old-fashioned look.

'No.'

She was relieved. She could just imagine what her mother would have thought if Milos had turned up there, unannounced.

'But I have been waiting here for you since—oh—' he glanced at his watch '—about a quarter past eight, I guess.'

Helen stared at him in disbelief. 'Why would you wait two hours to see me?'

Once again, Milos's expression told her what he thought of her question. But he chose not to provoke her. 'I thought it was time we talked,' he said. 'We've succeeded in avoiding the issue so far, but, hopefully, we'll have no interruptions tonight.'

Now Helen's whole body stiffened. 'C-couldn't it have waited until the morning?' she asked, unbuttoning her jacket and then buttoning it again. 'I am rather tired.'

'I can see that.' He didn't spare her. 'This has

been a traumatic time for you; I know that.' He paused. 'How is your mother, by the way? We heard she was much better.'

'We?' Helen swallowed. 'Who's we?'

'Your father, Melissa and me. Sam phoned the hospital this morning before I left. They said she was progressing well.'

'Then you don't need me to tell you how she is,' said Helen tartly, reaching for the kettle and carrying it to the sink. 'I'm going to make myself some tea. Do you want some?'

'How could I refuse such a generous offer?' he remarked drily. 'Then can we get to the point of this visit? I'm pretty tired—and cold—myself.'

'Oh!' Helen realised she hadn't given a thought to the fact that it was a cool, drizzly evening outside and he was used to temperatures in the seventies, at least. 'I'm sorry. Would you like me to put the heating on?'

'That won't be necessary,' Milos assured her. 'A drink will suffice just as well.'

'Well, we don't have anything alcoholic, I'm afraid.'

'As I say, tea will do,' he said, his irritation showing now. Then, with a frown, 'Have you had anything to eat this evening?'

Helen shrugged. 'I've had a sandwich.'

'A sandwich?' Milos sounded disgusted. 'And have you been living on sandwiches since you got back?'

Helen pursed her lips. 'I think that's my affair, don't you? Just because you think we have some unfinished business—'

'I don't think it,' he snapped, and she was briefly stunned by the anguish in his face. '*Theos*, Helen, how much longer do you think you can go on with this?'

'On with what?'

'Don't—don't pretend you don't know what I'm talking about.'

'I don't.'

'You're a liar,' he said harshly. He took a deep breath. 'Were you ever going to tell me that Melissa's my daughter?'

Helen's jaw sagged. 'Wh—what did you say?'

'I asked when you were going to tell me that I'm Melissa's father,' he said roughly. 'You needn't deny it. I've known for a while. Did you honestly think you could bring her to Santoros without me seeing the resemblance for myself?'

Helen had to sit down. Groping for one of the ladder-backed chairs that were set around the dinette table, she sank into it before her legs gave out on her completely. He knew, she thought despairingly. He knew Melissa was his daughter. Oh, God, had he told her, too?

The kettle was boiling, but Helen didn't have the strength to deal with it. With a muffled oath, Milos brushed past her. 'Tea?' he demanded, looking back at her, and she gestured shakily towards the tea caddy.

'There are teabags in there,' she said. 'The—the teapot's beside it.'

'I can see that.' He spoke flatly, and with enviable sureness he dropped a couple of bags into the pot and scalded them with the boiling water. 'Okay,' he said. 'Milk and sugar?'

By the time he pushed a mug of the hot beverage towards her, Helen was feeling strong enough to lift it to her lips and take a restoring sip. It was good, and reviving, and when Milos pulled out the chair opposite and straddled it she was able to look at him without breaking down.

'Have—have you told Melissa?' she asked, unable to prevent the question, and Milos regarded her with dark, accusing eyes.

'I suppose that is what you'd expect me to do,'

he said coldly. 'After all, I'm the man who got you pregnant and abandoned you.'

Helen trembled. 'So—so did you?'

'Tell Melissa?' She nodded and his lips twisted contemptuously. '*Fisika okhi!* Of course not. Contrary to the opinion you evidently have of me, I respect you too much for that. Though why I should after everything that's happened quite frankly amazes me.'

Helen moistened her lips. 'Thank you.'

Milos swore then and she started back in some alarm. 'Is that all you have to say?' he demanded. 'Thank you? *Theos*, Helen, don't you think I deserve more than that?'

Helen's eyes flickered to his and away again. 'I'm not going to apologise for what I did,' she said huskily. 'I thought you were married, remember?'

'How could I forget?' Milos scowled, his hands flexing and unflexing against the back of the chair. 'I haven't forgotten Eleni's part in this. If I had, you'd be facing something more than my anger, believe me.'

Helen shook her head. 'Is there any point in trying to explain why—why I did what I did and married Richard?'

'I'm listening, aren't I?'

'I suppose.' She sighed. 'It seemed the only solution. Richard was willing to marry me, and I
took the easy way out.'

'And did Shaw believe you were expecting
his child?' demanded Milos harshly, and Helen
flinched.

'No! He knew it wasn't—*she* wasn't. Richard
was my boyfriend, but we'd never slept together.'
She bent her head. 'But you know that.'

'Yeah.' Milos's scowl deepened. 'So when did
he change his mind?'

'Change his mind?' Helen was confused.
'Change his mind about what?'

'About his role as Melissa's father. When did he
decide to tell her the truth?'

Helen was stunned. 'He didn't. He wouldn't.'
She licked her dry lips. 'I don't know what you're
talking about. Melissa still believes Richard was
her father.'

'No.' Milos's denial was earth-shattering. 'No,
she doesn't.'

Helen could sit still no longer. Whereas before she'd felt weak and enervated, now agitation was giving her a panicky kind of energy that
demanded release. Pacing from one side of the
kitchen to the other, she tried to come to terms

with what he'd told her. But she couldn't believe it. Wouldn't believe it. Why would Richard do a thing like that? And if he had, why hadn't Melissa ever mentioned it to her?

Pressing her hands together, she considered the alternatives. As far as she knew, her mother had never doubted Melissa's parentage. Hadn't she always complained that she was her father's daughter, particularly when she was getting into trouble at school?

Which reminded her of how Richard had always refused to accept any responsibility for Melissa's behaviour. Despite maintaining an outward appearance of unity, in the privacy of their bedroom he'd never left Helen in any doubt that he blamed her for Melissa's attitude.

An attitude that had grown so much worse in recent months, Helen remembered anxiously. Oh, God, could it possibly be true? Had Richard told Melissa she was the illegitimate result of some liaison her mother had had before—or even after—they were married?

Recrossing the room again so that she could look into Milos's face, Helen chose her words with care. 'How—how do you know this?' She expelled an unsteady breath. 'Not that I'm saying I believe you, of course. But who would tell you such a thing?'

'Who do you think?'

Helen blinked. 'Not—my mother?'

'How could she?' Milos quickly got tired of her questions. 'It was Melissa herself. She told me.'

'No!' Helen stared at him in total disbelief. Then other, equally disturbing, thoughts occurred to her. 'Why would she tell you something like that?'

Milos blew out a breath. 'Well, not for the reasons you're considering,' he replied flatly. 'And, yes, believe me, I was tempted to tell her who her father really was. But, as I said before, I couldn't do it. Much as I want to acknowledge her, that information has to come from you, not me.'

Helen felt dazed. She couldn't take it all in. Her brain was scrambling to try and assimilate what he'd said. Melissa knew; she knew she wasn't Richard's daughter. Dear God, when had her late husband dropped that particular pearl of wisdom? Could it conceivably be the reason why Melissa's behaviour had become so uncontrollable in recent years?

'Did she tell you when he told her this?' she asked now, effectively accepting that Milos was telling her the truth.

'About two years ago.' Milos loosened the buttons on his suede jacket and rested his chin on his folded arms. 'She says he warned her not to tell you.'

'But why?' The cry was wrung from her. 'Why would he do a thing like that?'

'Bitterness? Jealousy? Melissa says he threatened to leave if she so much as hinted that she knew the truth.' He arched a weary brow. 'Way to go, Helen. He sounds like a prince.'

Helen shook her head. 'He was good to me in the beginning,' she protested. 'When Melissa was a baby, he seemed happy enough.'

'Were you?' asked Milos, looking up at her. 'Did you never wonder how different it would have been if we'd stayed together?'

Helen gave a scornful laugh. 'Like that was ever going to happen,' she exclaimed. 'Whether you'd known I was having your baby or not.'

'Why not?' Milos swung the chair aside and got to his feet. 'Was I such a hopeless prospect?'

'Oh, don't be ridiculous!' Helen turned away, unable to look at him when she felt so torn inside. 'I can just imagine the conversation if I'd rung and told you you were going to be a father.' She made an effort to imitate his horrified voice.

'*What? It can't be mine. I wore a condom. What trick are you trying to pull?*'

Milos made a bitter sound. 'That's some opinion you have of me.'

'Had. Had.' Helen couldn't honestly say she had the same opinion now. Not after the way he'd come to her with Melissa's confession. 'But, in any case, my opinion isn't important. Not now.' She bent her head. 'You see, I'd always thought you worked for my father, whereas—whereas—you don't.'

'And that's significant?'

He was behind her now. She could feel the warm draught of his breath on the back of her neck, feel the raw heat of his body sending shivers down her spine.

'What do you think?' she asked, trying to maintain her composure. And then, in a futile effort to distract him, she added, 'You still haven't told me how Melissa came to confide in you. I didn't think you knew one another that well.'

'Oh, we've come to know one another better since I got back from Athens,' said Milos softly, his hand skimming the shoulders of her jacket and causing her to flinch. 'When I discovered you'd gone back to England, it was an opportunity I couldn't miss.'

'I'll bet,' muttered Helen bitterly, and heard his sudden intake of breath.

'Do you blame me?' he asked, his fingers straying to the curve of her neck with disturbing familiarity. 'You may not like it, but Melissa and I seem to get along very well.'

Helen caught her breath. 'I'm surprised my father encouraged you,' she said. 'Didn't he think it was a little strange that you wanted to spend time with her?'

Milos sighed. 'It wasn't quite like that,' he said. 'I had the excuse that I wanted to see Rhea. She's been staying at the vineyard, keeping Melissa company while you've been away.'

'I see.' Helen tried not to be distracted by his provocative fingers. 'That was kind of her,' she said, the word escaping on a nervous gasp.

'Rhea is kind,' said Milos, his thumb finding the pulse that fluttered just below her ear. 'All the Stephanideses can be kind—if you let them.'

'That includes you, I suppose.'

'Especially me,' Milos agreed, tipping her head back until it rested against his shoulder. 'Do you want me to prove it?'

'That won't be necessary.' Twisting away, Helen put some much-needed space between them. 'Just tell me what you want from me,' she added, wrapping protective arms about her waist. 'I'm tired. It's too late to be playing word games.'

'It's no game,' said Milos flatly, regarding her with narrowed eyes. 'I thought you might be glad to see me. Apparently I was wrong.'

Helen shook her head. 'If you mean because of what happened at Vassilios—'

'Of course I mean because of what happened at Vassilios,' he broke in harshly. '*Theos*, how could you have any doubts?'

Helen took a trembling breath. 'I thought you came to tell me that you knew about Melissa.'

'That, too. And to ask if you knew about what your husband had said.'

'I didn't.'

'Don't worry. I believe you.' His scowl appeared. 'But I dared to think we had other things to talk about. Or am I being totally insensitive? I guess your mother's accident hasn't left much room for anything else.'

Helen quivered. If he only knew!

'You—you still haven't told me how Melissa came to confide in you,' she said, unable to voice how she was really feeling, and then gulped when Milos uttered an anguished cry.

'Goddammit,' he said, 'can't you forget about Melissa, just for a moment? I'm tired, too, but I'm not going anywhere until we have a chance to talk about us!'

'Us?' she echoed faintly. Her heart was hammering crazily against her ribs.

'Yes, us,' said Milos thickly, reaching for her. His hand caught her face, tipping it up to him. Then he covered her mouth with his.

She hadn't expected him to kiss her. Indeed, there had been such fire in his eyes that she hadn't known what he intended. In consequence, she wasn't prepared for it, wasn't ready for the hot wet passion that consumed her or the hungry tongue he thrust into her mouth. She had no will, no barriers to raise against him, and he plundered her lips with all the heat and sensuality of his nature.

Her head swam and she clutched him helplessly, needing his strength to prevent her from collapsing at his feet. He parted his legs to draw her closer and almost of its own volition her body curled into his, seeking his warmth and protection, with the wanton need she'd been denying for so long.

The kiss seemed to go on for ever and they were both panting and breathless when Milos finally lifted his head. '*Theos*,' he said hoarsely, 'you drive me crazy!' And then, with another muffled oath, he stepped back and raked both hands through his hair.

Helen stood there feeling totally bereft. For a moment, she had forgotten everything: the reasons he'd given her for being here, her mother's accident; even her own grounds for not trusting him. Her lips felt swollen, and any make-up she'd been wearing had probably transferred itself to his mouth. But she realised now it hadn't meant anything. He'd been angry and he'd punished her in the only way he knew how.

'Go on,' he said. 'Tell me I'm a bastard. That is what you're thinking, isn't it? It's what you've always thought about me.'

'You're wrong.' Helen chose her words with care. 'I just don't know why you did it.' She paused. 'Do you hate me so much?'

'I don't hate you!' Milos groaned, cupping the back of his neck with both hands, his jacket swinging open over his flat stomach. She knew his stomach was taut and hard and liberally ribbed with muscle. She'd felt it when he'd pulled her against him. She knew she'd also detected the hardening pressure in his groin when he'd thrust his thigh between her shaking legs. 'I sometimes wish I did.'

'Then—'

'Look, I'll tell you about Melissa, if that's what you want,' he muttered, before she could go on. Groping behind him for the chair he'd been straddling earlier, he dropped down into it, propping his elbows on his knees, his chin cradled between his cupped hands. 'The night I got back from Athens, Rhea persuaded Sam to let the two girls spend the night at Vassilios. I couldn't sleep because—well, because I couldn't sleep, okay? Melissa couldn't either, so—we talked.'

Helen wished she had a chair to sit on, too, but she stayed where she was. 'What did you talk about?' she asked, wishing she didn't feel such a need to protect him. He looked so weary, she thought. She couldn't help worrying about how long it was since he'd shaved or slept, or had something to eat.

Milos grimaced now. 'What do you think we talked about?' he asked, and with difficulty she tried to concentrate on what he was saying. 'You; her grandmother; the accident. She was concerned that the old lady might be going to die. She said that you and your mother were the only two people who really cared about her.' His lips twisted. 'And how do you think that made me feel?'

Helen could imagine. 'Pretty bad,' she murmured, and he gave her a telling look.

'At least,' he said. 'So I compromised my beliefs by asking about *her father*. I said it must be hard having to deal with another accident so soon after her father had died.'

Helen swallowed. 'And she said?'

'That Richard wasn't her father,' said Milos grimly. 'I guess she's been wanting to tell someone that for a long time.'

'Oh, God!' Helen pressed her hands to her cheeks. 'I wish I'd known.'

'So do I,' said Milos bitterly. 'But we don't always get what we want, do we?'

Helen felt devastated. More devastated than she'd felt when he'd first revealed what Melissa had said. She was unhappily aware that she was to blame, much more than he was. She'd been so busy trying to hold the family together that she'd lost sight of what was going on right under her nose.

'I'm sorry,' she said, trembling as she stood

in front of him. 'You've every right to be angry with me.'

Milos groaned. 'I'm not angry with you,' he protested, reaching out once again and capturing her hand. He pulled her to stand between his spread thighs. 'But you realise now why I couldn't wait for you to come back to Santoros. I had to talk to you. I had to tell you.'

Helen hesitated. 'I—I may not be able to come back to Santoros,' she said. 'My mother's being released from hospital in a day or two, and I've got to be here for her.'

Milos gave a heavy sigh. 'That's what I was afraid of,' he said flatly. He carried her hand to his lips and pressed his mouth against her palm. 'So—I need you to assure me that you'll tell Melissa that I'm her father when—when she gets back from the island. Not immediately, perhaps.' She felt his tongue only moments before he added. 'But I think you owe me that, if nothing else.'

Helen nodded. 'I'll tell her.'

'Thank you.' Milos looked up at her wearily. 'Would you believe me if I told you something else?'

Helen shivered, her whole being concentrated on his face. His hand gripping hers made her intensely aware of the connection between them, and, while she could tell herself this was just another game he was playing, she knew she'd never forgive herself if she was wrong.

'Try me,' she said, her breasts tightening in anticipation. There was an ache in the pit of her stomach and, in spite of herself, moisture was pooling between her legs. She tried telling herself he was only here because he wanted something from her, but the truth was he'd confounded every preconception she'd had about him so far.

'Okay.' Milos took both of her hands in his now and drew her closer. 'I hoped we might be able to salvage something from the mess I've made of both our lives.'

Helen caught her breath. 'You don't have to do this, you know.'

Milos frowned now. 'Do what?'

'Pretend that you're attracted to me, to persuade me to let you have access to Melissa.' Helen held up her head. 'She's your daughter, Milos. You have every right to demand an equal share of her time.'

There was silence for a moment, and then Milos pushed Helen away and got abruptly to his feet. 'You—' He bit back an expletive, raking his scalp with shaking fingers. 'Do you honestly think I'd go so far as to make love to you to force you to acknowledge the truth?'

Helen's legs felt decidedly unsteady. 'I don't know what to think, do I?' she defended herself. 'I don't know you well enough to decide.'

'Then perhaps you should,' said Milos, brushing past her. 'Look, I've got to go. It's getting late and I'm dead on my feet. Maybe we can talk again tomorrow. I'll give you a ring in the morning. When I've got my head together. When what I'm saying makes a little more sense.'

'Milos...' Helen said his name and then, guessing he might misunderstand, she added quickly, 'You don't have to go. Not if you don't want to. I mean—we have plenty of spare beds here.'

Milos paused in the doorway, his shoulders wedged against the frame of one side, his hand braced to support himself against the other. 'You can't be serious,' he said harshly. 'You don't honestly think I could share a house with you without sharing your bed?' He shook his head impatiently. 'Talk sense, Helen. After what I just said, you can't calmly offer me a bed for the night!'

Helen's pulse was racing. 'Why not?'

Milos repeated roughly. 'You know why not.

Theos, Helen, do you think I could have forgiven you for depriving me of the first twelve years of my daughter's life if I didn't care about you? I'm not a saint, Helen. I'm a sinner. I wanted you when you were too young and innocent to know better, and I want you still. That's my excuse?'

Helen was stunned. 'Then—then why didn't you say so?'

'When?' He pushed away from the door, but to her relief he didn't walk away from her. 'When you were trying to make me jealous with your rich boyfriend, or when you were fighting me like a tigress, that morning at Vassilios?'

Helen only heard one thing. 'I—I wasn't trying to make you jealous,' she protested, gazing at him incredulously. 'I wouldn't do a thing like that.' She hesitated. 'I care about you too much.'

Milos halted in front of her. 'And I'm supposed to believe that?'

'Yes. Yes. It's the truth.' Helen hesitated only a moment before covering the space between them. 'You've got to believe me,' she said, gazing up at him with wide, appealing eyes. She grasped his arm, revelling in the unaccustomed freedom of being able to express her feelings at last. 'Did you mean what you said? You really do want me?'

'I really do.' Milos's fingers closed around her arms, jerking her towards him. 'Crazy woman,' he added, flicking her lips with his tongue. 'What a lot of time we've wasted, you and I.'

Helen didn't know what he meant by that. Whether he wanted her as his mistress or something else she didn't dare think about, she didn't care. It was enough that he was holding her, that his mouth was doing erotic things to hers. She'd worry about the future when she'd learned to let go of the past.

She moaned as his tongue plunged deeply into her mouth, desire snaking like a fire through her belly. His hands were on her hips now, urging her more closely against him, letting her feel his throbbing arousal as he rubbed himself sensuously against her crotch.

Somehow, her skirt had ridden up her legs, and Milos's hands moved to cup the bare backs of her thighs. She was so glad she was wearing stockings and not tights, particularly when his fingertips probed the sensitive heat between her legs.

'You're wet,' he said thickly, and she was too aroused to feel any embarrassment at his invasion.

'You do that to me,' she said instead, and his triumphant laugh was muffled against her throat.

'You really want me,' he said, opening the buttons of her shirt and exposing the lacy cups of her bra. 'But you wear too many clothes,' he added gruffly. 'What was that you said about offering me a bed for the night?'

CHAPTER FIFTEEN

HOURS later, Milos was awakened by Helen climbing onto the bed beside him. He'd slept, he realised, feeling an unaccustomed sense of relaxation. And a delicious sense of satisfaction. He couldn't remember ever feeling as content as he felt at this moment.

Because of Helen...

Blinking in the pale light filtering through the drawn curtains, he saw she'd placed a tray of tea on the bedside table. She'd also dressed in some silky clinging garment that exposed her cleavage and gave tantalising glimpses of her bare thighs.

Immediately, his body responded, and a rush of heat invaded his groin. Just the smell of her skin and he could feel the need stirring inside him, a carnal need that caused a physical ache in his gut.

'I've brought you some tea,' she said, and judging by the breathy catch in her voice she was as aware of his erection as he was. 'Not the tea you made,' she added huskily. 'That was stone cold.'

'Unlike me,' he said drily, pushing himself up on his elbows. 'What time is it? It can't be morning already.'

'I'm afraid it is.' Helen's smile was rueful. 'It's nearly eight o'clock.'

'Like I said, it's not morning yet,' he retorted, reaching out to grasp a handful of her robe. 'Mmm, this feels nice. Take it off.'

Helen's lips parted. 'I can't.'

'Yes, you can,' he said, watching her with heavy-lidded eyes. And although she obviously wasn't used to undressing in front of anyone, she obediently unfastened the cord at her waist and let the robe hang free.

'Yeah, that's much better,' he murmured approvingly, looping his hand behind her head. 'Now come here.'

Helen couldn't help herself. Milos covered her mouth with his and bore her back against the pillows so that her breasts were crushed against his chest. Although he'd pulled a sheet over them before they'd slept, it posed little problem when he kicked it aside.

The warmth of her slim, lissom body beneath him was all he needed to feel. A groan of pure pleasure vibrated in his chest as he parted her legs with his thigh and pressed his erection to the sensitive opening of her body.

'Do you know how much I love you?' he demanded, tantalising her and himself by not penetrating the moist coils that he knew awaited him, and she uttered a little moan of protest.

'Don't tease me,' she cried, reaching down between them to aid his passage, and Milos made a choking sound of defeat. The devastating brush of her cool fingers over his hot, pulsating shaft almost sent him over the edge, and with a muffled oath of submission he thrust into her yielding flesh.

Only to draw back again in sudden awareness. 'I don't have any protection,' he muttered, but she only wound her legs about his waist and urged him on.

'Do you care?' she breathed, her tongue circling his lips, her fingers shivering over the roughening stubble on his jaw line. 'Just do it, Milos. You know you want to.'

He had no argument with that, thought Milos roughly, plunging into her again and feeling her slick muscles closing about him. He half hoped he did make her pregnant. It was one way of ensuring that they'd stay together, and right now that was all he cared about.

He climaxed a few moments later with the aftermath of Helen's orgasm still rippling through her body. He spilled himself into her, shuddering at the force of his emotions. He'd never experienced anything like the feelings Helen aroused in him, and he would have been quite content to spend the rest of the day in bed.

But minutes later Helen was wriggling out from under him. 'I'm sorry,' she said, stroking his cheek when he would have detained her, 'but I've got to go.'

'Where?' Milos scowled. 'It's too early for visiting the hospital, isn't it?'

She dimpled. 'I have to go to work, to see Mark. I have to tell him I'll need at least another week off.'

'Mark?' Milos's scowl deepened. 'Mark who?'

'Mark Greenaway,' replied Helen lightly, reaching for her robe and slipping it over her shoulders. 'He's my boss. He's been very good to me since Richard died. He knew I was going to be away for a couple of weeks, but now I need more time to look after my mother when she gets home.'

Milos's jaw compressed. 'Is he married?'

'Mark?' Helen cheeks turned a little pink. 'No.'

'Is he the rich boyfriend Melissa spoke about?'

Helen tried to wrap her robe about her and get off the bed, but he was too quick for her. 'Is he?' he persisted, aware of a most unfamiliar feeling of rage at the idea. 'I want to know.'

Helen sighed. 'He—cares about me, yes.'

Milos blew out a breath. 'Has he asked you to marry him?'

Helen gasped. 'Does it matter?'

'Of course, it matters.' Milos brought her fingers to his lips. 'I want to know what the competition is.'

Helen shook her head, a little sadly, he thought. 'There is no competition,' she said huskily. 'I thought you knew that.'

Milos absorbed this. 'So if I'd asked you to marry me? What then?'

Helen trembled. 'But you haven't asked,' she pointed out softly, turning away and concentrating on the ties of her robe that had become trapped between her legs. 'And I don't want you to do something you might regret just because you think I might be attracted by Mark's proposal. I won't. I've turned him down once and I'd turn him down again, whatever happens.'

Milos expelled a sigh of relief. 'I've done all the regretting I'm going to do,' he said feelingly. Then, getting onto his knees, he caught her chin and brought her round to face him. 'So will you? Marry me, I mean? It's what I want, more than anything else.'

They flew back to Santoros in Milos's private plane two days later.

Helen's mother was installed in the back of the plane in the double bed that Milos sometimes used on long-haul journeys, and with an agency nurse on hand to attend to her every need. Milos wasn't sure how she felt about the fact that her daughter had agreed to marry one of her ex-husband's associates, but thankfully she'd agreed to being transported to Milos's villa to complete her recuperation. Maybe she'd realised that, as Milos was a wealthy man, her life was going to be considerably easier from now on. Whatever, he was cynically aware that Sheila's attitude had changed as soon as she'd discovered who he was, and he wasn't averse to looking a gift horse in the mouth.

So long as Helen was happy, that was all that mattered to him. And she was, deliriously so, and she'd given in her notice at Greenaway Engineering.

She'd gone on her own to tell Mark Greenaway. Even though Milos had desperately wanted to go with her, to stake his claim so to speak, he'd contained his jealousy and let her go alone. He wanted her to know he trusted her just as much as she trusted him.

Naturally, they'd told no one about Melissa. Until Helen had spoken to Melissa herself, that would remain a secret. Milos had no idea how the girl would take it, but, whatever happened, they were a family now and that had to mean something. Especially to her.

The Jetstream landed at the nearest airport to Santoros, and Milos's helicopter was waiting to transport them the last few miles to the island.

'Tired?' he asked his fiancée gently, catching her hand as she was about to follow her mother up the steps and into the aircraft. He was mindful of the fact that the last couple of nights they'd spent together had hardly been restful, and he blamed himself for the half-moons of darkness that marred her soft cheeks. 'We'll be there soon.'

'No more tired than you,' she told him huskily, reaching up to bestow a warm kiss at the corner of his mouth. 'I ache a bit, perhaps. But it's a good ache. I like it.'

The rush Milos felt then was purely carnal, and his fingers dug into her palm. 'You shouldn't say things like that when I can't do anything about them,' he told her unevenly. His eyes darkened. 'I can't wait to show you our bedroom at the villa.'

'Would that be *your* bedroom?' asked Helen primly, and he couldn't prevent himself from nipping her bottom as she went up the steps.

'No, that would be *our* bedroom,' he corrected her thickly. 'Go on. Your mother's waiting.'

Melissa was waiting for them at Vassilios. She and Stelios came to greet them as soon as the helicopter touched down. The pilot let down the steps and Milos went ahead to assist his future mother-in-law to alight. Sheila looked a little tired, too, he noticed with some concern, but then Melissa saw them and came running towards them.

'Hey, Gran,' she exclaimed, offering Milos a bright smile of welcome, too, before giving her grandmother a swift hug. 'Travelling in style, eh?'

Sheila patted Melissa's shoulder. 'Yes, wasn't it kind of Milos to offer me his villa to recuperate in? Still, I suppose I'll get used to coming here from now on.'

Melissa looked puzzled. 'Will you?' she said, looking at Milos a little confusedly. And then, remembering her manners, she added, 'So, how are you? Is your arm really broken?'

'It's really broken,' agreed Sheila smugly as Milos endeavoured to catch her eye. But she seemed determined not to look at him and he waited apprehensively for her to say something she shouldn't.

Then, to his relief, Helen emerged from the helicopter just ahead of the nurse, and Melissa hesitated only a moment before going to meet her mother. But Milos saw her glance curiously over her shoulder as she went and he was briefly reminded of the problems Sam had said he'd had with his ex-wife.

'We haven't told Melissa about our engagement yet,' he said quickly, in a low voice, and Sheila glanced up at him with wide, enquiring eyes.

'Why not?'

'We haven't had the chance.'

'There are telephones on Santoros, aren't there?' Sheila was irritatingly precise. 'You might even have cell phones, for all I know.'

'We wanted to tell her together,' said Milos, between his teeth. 'Do me—do us both the favour

of keeping our relationship to yourself. At least
for the time being.'

Sheila arched a mocking brow. 'Was this Helen's
idea? To keep your relationship a secret? Or
yours?'

'It's not a secret,' said Milos grimly. 'We intend
to tell her tonight.'

'If you say so.' Sheila sounded uninterested now,
casting a glance about her, her eyes alighting on
Stelios where he hovered a few yards away. 'Is
that your butler, Milos? I'd be grateful if he could
show me to my room.'

Milos hid a smile at the thought of what Stelios
would think of being called a 'butler'. But it was
a relief to have an excuse to usher the woman
into the house. Susie Peel, Sheila's nurse, hurried
to join them, and by the time Helen and Melissa
reached him the others were already crossing the
terrace.

'Is Mum staying here, too?' asked Melissa as
the three of them started towards the villa.

Helen cast a quick look at Milos before saying,
'I thought I might.'

'Oh, good. That means I can stay here, too,
doesn't it?' Melissa asked, looking up at Milos.

'I don't know what Sam's going to say, but I expect he'll get over it.'

'Well, he wouldn't want your gran staying with him,' murmured Helen drily, and felt Milos's hand brush reassuringly against hers as they reached the entrance to the villa.

'No, I guess not.' Melissa grimaced. 'Oh, well, would you mind if I went and told Gran what's going on? I want to see what she thinks of her room. Andrea's given her a super view, right on the sea.'

Helen looked at Milos for confirmation. 'That would be okay, wouldn't it?' she said. 'Then perhaps you could show me where I'm going to sleep.'

Melissa halted then. 'Yeah, I'd like to see that, too,' she said. 'I expect it's one of the rooms near mine. But all the rooms are beautiful here,' she appended, half enviously. 'Go figure.'

'Why don't you go and find Andrea instead and ask her what time she expects to serve lunch?' Milos suggested, in no hurry to push Melissa into her grandmother's company again. 'You can see your grandmother after she gets settled in.'

Melissa's lips pursed for a moment. 'Why?' she asked, with a trace of her previous belligerence. 'Is there some reason why I shouldn't go and see her?' She hesitated. 'She is okay, isn't she? She's not going to—like, die, or anything?'

'Of course not,' said Helen, and Milos could see she, too, was puzzled by his attitude. 'But if that's what—Milos wants you to do—'

'Oh, all right.' But Melissa was sulky now. 'I just hope I'm not going to have to stick to a whole lot of rules while we're staying here. If so, I'd rather go back to the vineyard. Even if Maya hates me.'

'Maya doesn't hate you,' said Helen at once, and Milos decided it was time he told them both something they needed to know.

'Maya's not so bad when you get to know her,' he said levelly. 'But the vineyard's important to her, and when you and your mother turned up she was afraid that Sam might change his mind about leaving it to Alex.'

Melissa's jaw dropped. 'You mean she's afraid Sam might make Mum his heir?'

'Something like that,' agreed Milos, unable to resist laying a possessive hand on Helen's shoulder, but Melissa didn't notice. She was too intent on what he'd said.

'But that's silly,' she said. 'Mum knows nothing

about growing grapes or making wine, whereas
Alex has done it all his life.'

'That's right.' Milos nodded.

'I had no idea,' said Helen then, and he could
tell she'd been stunned by his revelation. 'So that
was why—'

'She was so keen to get rid of you?' Milos pulled
a wry face. 'Like someone else I know, she's inclined to speak out of turn.'

'Do you mean me?' demanded Melissa indignantly, but Milos only reached out and tugged on
the fringe that now strayed across her forehead.

'No,' he said gently. 'Now, are you going to go
and see Andrea, as I requested?'

When Melissa had left them, Milos swiftly drew
Helen into his study. Then, after closing and lock-
ing the door, he pulled her into his arms and buried his face in the scented hollow of her shoulder.

'*Theos*, I needed that,' he said, when he lifted
his head to look down at her. 'You have no idea
how much.'

Helen was nothing if not perceptive. 'What's
wrong?' she asked. 'Has something happened?'
She paused. 'Sam isn't creating problems, is he?'

'Well, not yet,' said Milos drily. 'How he'll feel
when I tell him about Melissa is another matter.'

'I'll tell him,' Helen offered at once, but Milos shook his head.

'No. I have to do that,' he said determinedly. 'That's my problem. Your mother is ours.'

Helen's shoulders sagged. 'What did she do?'

'She was on the verge of telling Melissa about us.' He grimaced. 'Don't worry, I stopped her.'

'So you think we should tell Melissa straight away?'

'As soon as possible,' agreed Milos, tucking a strand of silky blonde hair behind her ear. 'Thank God Sheila doesn't know about anything else.'

'Amen to that,' said Helen fervently. 'What do I say when she—Melissa—asks where my room is?'

'Good question.' Milos's lips twitched. 'Well, as she doesn't know where my suite is, I don't think that's going to be a problem. Not until tomorrow morning, perhaps.'

'When she might find us together?' asked Helen tentatively, and Milos pulled a wry face.

'When she'll definitely find us together,' he assured her roughly, and Helen lifted her face for his kiss.

* * *

Helen was unpacking her belongings when Melissa came to find her.

Milos had left, ostensibly to visit Rhea, but in fact, he was going to see Sam. They didn't dare give Helen's mother the chance to pre-empt their news, and taunting her ex-husband with such privileged information would obviously sour their relationship with him.

Melissa came into Milos's apartment, whistling admiringly as she looked about her. 'Hey, this is some room,' she said, approaching the huge bed and bouncing on the edge for a moment. 'Milos must really want to impress you.'

Helen's cheeks turned a little pink. 'It is nice, isn't it?' she admitted. She moistened her lips. 'Is your room far away?'

'About as far away as you could get it,' said Melissa drily. 'I'm in the opposite wing, near where they've put Gran.' She paused. 'What was all that before about me waiting until she was settled before I went to see her? It was like Milos was afraid I'd say something I shouldn't.' She spread her hands. 'I just wish I knew what.'

'I'm sure Milos didn't mean anything like that,' said Helen quickly, thinking how easy it was to get completely the wrong idea. 'He was probably just thinking of your gran, that's all.'

'You think?' Melissa considered this for a moment and then she said shrewdly, 'Anyway, you two seem to be getting along better these days. I mean, like, I was totally shocked when Rhea said she thought that you and Gran were going to be staying here.'

Helen expelled a nervous breath. 'Well, it just seemed the best solution,' she said awkwardly. 'And you must admit, there is a lot more room here.'

'Oh, yeah.' Melissa flopped down onto the bed again, watching as her mother laid the clothes she had taken from her suitcases onto the ottoman at its foot. 'Hey, isn't that my tee shirt? And those are my canvas trousers. Why have you brought them?'

'I just thought you might need them,' said her mother steadily. 'As we're going to be staying much longer than we'd originally planned.'

'Mmm.'

Melissa seemed to absorb this, but then to Helen's dismay she sprang up from the bed again and went to pull open the door into the walk-in closet. 'You might as well put your clothes in here,' she was beginning, when she stopped dead, turning back to look at her mother with accusing eyes. 'Hey, there are clothes in here already. Men's clothes.'

Helen's heart sank, but she had to be honest. 'I know.'

Melissa's brows drew together. 'They're Milos's clothes,' she said, evidently recognising something of his. Then, turning back to her mother again, 'What's going on? Why are Milos's clothes in here?'

Helen shook her head. 'I expect he left them there,' she said tiredly. 'This is his room, after all.'

'Wow!' Melissa stared at her. 'You mean, he's given up his own room for you?'

Helen sighed. 'Something like that,' she said, wishing Milos were here at this moment.

'Man!' Melissa was obviously impressed. Then, as her natural intelligence kicked in, she blinked disbelievingly. 'Don't tell me you two are an item!'

Helen hesitated. It wasn't the most ideal way to tell her, but she was sure Milos wouldn't blame her. 'Would you mind if we were?' she asked huskily, and Melissa gave an incredulous whoop of excitement.

'Are you kidding?' she exclaimed. 'Does that mean we get to live on Santoros for good?'

'No.'

'Why not?'

'Because Milos spends part of his time in Athens. He has—business interests there.'

'Oil-tankers, I know. He told me,' said Melissa impatiently, and Helen remembered that awful journey from the ferry to her father's house as if it were yesterday. 'Well, that doesn't matter. Athens is good, too.'

'I'm glad you approve.'

'So it's true?' Melissa had to have chapter and verse. 'Are you and Milos sleeping together?'

'Melissa!' Helen was shocked at her daughter's casual acceptance of something that when she'd been her age had been regarded so differently.

'Well, are you?'

Melissa was waiting for an answer and Helen couldn't do anything else but admit that they were. 'But we're going to get married,' she added hastily, needing to legitimise the arrangement. 'As soon as Milos's parents get back from their cruise.'

'Hey, you don't have to tell me that,' said Melissa, coming round the bed and throwing an affectionate arm around her mother's neck. 'People don't need to get married to prove they love one another.' She grimaced. 'Anyway, I guessed what was going on. I'm not exactly naïve, you know?'

Helen gazed at her daughter with moist eyes. 'Thank you.'

'What are you thanking me for?'

Helen shook her head. 'I don't know. Just being you, I guess. You can be very sensitive sometimes, Mellie.'

'Don't call me Mellie,' exclaimed Melissa disgustedly, pulling a face. 'Anyway, wait until Milos gets back. I'm gonna ask him what his intentions are.'

Helen was horrified. 'Don't you dare!'

Melissa giggled. 'Why not? He's going to be my father, isn't he?'

'Well, yes.' Helen hesitated. 'About your father—'

'You mean Richard.'

'All right, Richard, then.' Helen bit her lip. 'Milos told me—oh, Melissa, why didn't you come to see me when Richard told you he wasn't your father?'

'If Milos has talked to you, you know why.'

'But you were more important to me than

Richard,' protested Helen fiercely. 'And if I'd known what he'd told you, I'd have left him, never mind the other way around.'

'Would you?' Melissa was gazing at her anxiously now, and Helen suddenly realised how much Richard's words had sapped the child's confidence.

'Of course, I would,' she exclaimed, pulling Melissa into her arms and giving her a heartfelt hug. 'You were always the most important person in my world. I thought you knew that.'

Melissa sniffed. 'But you didn't love my real father, did you? I mean, if you had, you'd have married him, wouldn't you? Not Richard.' She paused. 'Unless he was already married. Was he already married, Mum? Was that why you couldn't marry him? Richard said I was just the result of a one-night stand and that you didn't even know who my father was.'

'Oh, God!' Helen was stunned. 'Of course I know who your father is. I—I was a virgin before—before we made you.'

'And was he married?'

It was very important to Melissa to believe he was and Helen couldn't be less than honest. Not now. 'I thought he was,' she admitted unhappily.

'I didn't find out I was wrong until—until quite recently.'

'So who is he?' asked Melissa eagerly. 'Tell me. Is it someone I know? Oh, God, it isn't Mark Greenaway, is it?'

'No.' Helen closed her eyes for a moment. 'It isn't Mark Greenaway.'

Melissa was obviously relieved. 'But is it someone I know?'

Helen shook her head. 'Who would you like it to be?' she asked, desperately seeking a way out, a way not to tell her until Milos was here, and Melissa frowned.

'You still don't want to tell me, do you?'

'I do, I do.' Helen made a helpless gesture. 'Just answer my question first.'

Melissa scowled, looking so like her father that Helen had to catch her breath. 'Well, let me see,' she muttered ill-humouredly. 'How about Prince Charles, hmm? Or maybe just Brad Pitt, though I guess his current lady wouldn't be too thrilled about that.'

'Melissa!'

'Oh, okay.' Melissa pulled away from her and walked across to the windows. Standing looking out at the view, she said carelessly, 'Well, I sup-

pose the most obvious person would be Milos.
I mean, he's young, he's good-looking, and he's
rich. And he obviously cares about you.'

Helen sucked in a breath. 'Good choice,' she
said, and Melissa cast a moody look over her
shoulder.

'Okay,' she said. 'You've had your fun. Now,
why don't you tell me who it really is?'

'Because you know,' said a blessedly familiar
voice behind them and Helen turned weakly to
find Milos strolling casually into the room. He
shed his jacket on the bed, and then, after giving
Helen an understanding look, he went to join his
daughter by the windows. 'Sorry to disappoint
you about the prince and so on, but it's me. It really is.'

Melissa's mouth opened in silent disbelief. Then,
closing it again, she said, 'You're kidding, right?'

Milos arched a dark brow. 'Do I look like I'm
kidding?'

'No.' The word whispered from her lips, and
Helen had to steel herself not to rush across the
room and take the girl into her arms. 'You—you're
my father? And you've known this—'

'Since a couple of days after you got here,' Milos

told her honestly. 'Believe me, it was a shock to me, too.'

Melissa shook her head, looking beyond him now to where her mother was still standing beside the bed. 'But you knew before that,' she said accusingly. 'You've known my whole life, and you've never told me.'

'I couldn't—' began Helen, wanting to explain that Richard had deceived her, too, but Melissa wouldn't let her go on.

'You knew,' she said again, putting her hands over her ears to block anything else anyone might say. 'You knew and you didn't tell me. Oh, my God! My God! Too much information!'

She was gone before either of them could stop her, rushing across the room and out the door, with tears streaming down her face. In the silence that followed her departure, Helen sank down onto the bed and buried her face in her hands.

'Oh, Lord,' she whispered, feeling as if the bottom had just dropped out of her world. 'Oh, Lord, she's never going to forgive me!'

'Of course, she will.' Milos was amazingly calm considering the circumstances. He came around the bed and put his arm about her, giving her a brief, but wonderfully reassuring, hug. Then, with a grin, he straightened again. 'Leave her to me, *agape mou*. Believe me, compared to your father, she'll be a pushover!'

Helen and Milos were married six weeks later in the small chapel on the Stephanides estate. The ceremony, a simple affair, was confined to their immediate family and friends, but many of the islanders turned out to wish their patron's son well.

Milos's mother would have preferred a much grander affair. She'd wanted them to get married at the cathedral in Athens, with all the pomp and circumstance that would have entailed.

However, she'd had to agree, somewhat grudgingly, that such a dispensation, bearing in mind that her son had been divorced, might have been difficult to arrange. Besides, neither Milos nor Helen had wanted to wait, and in the end Helen had had her way. A quiet wedding, where the words they had spoken had meant more than their surroundings.

Initially, Helen had been afraid that Milos's parents wouldn't like her; that they'd expect she was a gold-digger; that Melissa's existence would cause dismay and not delight. But she couldn't have been more wrong. Whatever they thought of her, their discovery that they had a ready-made granddaughter had swayed the balance. In a tearful moment, Athene had confessed that they'd both given up hope of Milos ever giving them any grandchildren. He'd always shunned any efforts they'd made to persuade him otherwise. But now she was prepared to accept that, however unlikely it seemed, he had been waiting for Helen to come back.

It was a nice thing to say, and, although Helen wasn't sure whether she or Athene believed it, it did augur well for the relationship they were bound to have in the years to come.

Helen's mother had taken the news very differently. With one of her smug smiles, she'd maintained that she'd guessed who Melissa's father was all along. She'd just never said anything because of Milos's association with her ex-husband.

Not that Helen had known this until much later. Hers and Milos's first thoughts had been for their daughter, and when they'd tracked her down to Helen's mother's room, and Melissa had announced in a choking voice that she'd already told her grandmother who Milos was, the atmosphere had been electric.

The stand-off had faltered somewhat when

Melissa had gone on to say that she didn't want to stay at Vassilios. She wanted to go and stay with her grandfather, she maintained, and nothing Helen, Milos or her grandmother could say would make her change her mind.

The upshot was that Milos himself had driven the girl to the vineyard, braving Sam's wrath for a second time that day. Helen's father had been reluctant to get involved, but Melissa was his granddaughter, after all. Responding to her pleas, he'd agreed to let her stay for a couple of nights.

Helen had been shattered when Milos had got back, a combination of her daughter's recalcitrance and her mother's self-satisfaction proving the last straw. She'd been convinced that nothing and no one could mend the breach that now yawned between her and her daughter, and she'd been distraught.

A week later, she was able to look back on those first days with disbelief. She'd calculated without Milos's involvement. For so long, she had had to make all the decisions concerning Melissa for herself, and having someone else shoulder the burden was such a relief.

She never did find out what he'd actually said to

their daughter to make her change her mind. She suspected he'd played on the fact that Melissa expected them to believe her when she said Richard had threatened her, yet she was unwilling to listen to her mother when she tried to tell her he had deceived her, too. Whatever, within a couple of days, Melissa was back at Vassilios with her grandfather's blessing, and the return of Milos's mother and father had successfully completed the reconciliation. Helen had no doubt there would be problems to come, maybe even another rebellion about their relationship, but she didn't doubt that, with Milos to support her, they would make it through.

The wedding itself was magical. Helen's father had agreed to escort her down the aisle, and with some inducement from her new grandparents Melissa had been prevailed upon to act as maid of honour.

Helen had been relieved to find her father's anger over Milos being Melissa's father hadn't lasted. The two men had been friends for so long, and she'd been afraid the animosity would spoil that. But, as with the peace Sam had made with his first wife, time had proved a great healer. The mistakes he'd made in his own life had helped him to understand Milos's dilemma and he accepted that Milos genuinely loved his daughter, and probably always had.

Everything had been so different from her first wedding, thought Helen later that night, standing at the rail of Milos's yacht. Then it had taken place in a register office, with Sheila Campbell and Richard's widowed mother as the only witnesses, the latter under duress.

They were spending their honeymoon cruising in the Mediterranean, while Melissa stayed at Vassilios with Rhea and Helen's mother. It was an arrangement that would enable her to get to know her new grandparents properly, and the girl was already blossoming under so much loving attention.

Helen's mother had been given the option of staying on the island or returning to England. With no financial worries, Sheila would be able to come and go as she pleased, and that obviously delighted her.

'You may regret that,' Helen had heard her father say drily to her husband, but Milos had assured the older man that Santoros was big enough for all of them.

'In any case, we—that is, Helen, Melissa and I—will be spending half the year in Athens,' he said blandly. 'Melissa has to go to school, you know.'

Helen had heard her father laugh at that, and, remembering, she thought how lucky she was to have two such wonderful men in her life.

'Happy?'

Milos had left the yacht in the charge of its efficient skipper and come to join her, and Helen leaned back against the warm strength of his shoulder.

'Blissfully,' she said happily. She tipped her head up to him. 'Are you?'

'Well, let me see.' Milos frowned, tipping the strap of her camisole off her shoulder as he did so. 'I'm married to the woman I've loved for most of my life and she loves me.' He bent his head and licked the warm skin he'd exposed before continuing, 'We have a teenage daughter, who, despite being a bit of a pain sometimes, is extremely precious to both of us, and will no doubt prove to be a great older sister to any future children we might have.' He nuzzled her neck. 'Yes, on balance, I'd say I was—very happy.'

'That's good.' Helen lifted her shoulder to his lips. 'But you know what you said about any future children?' She took a nervous breath. 'We might not have to wait too long to find out.'

Milos swung her round to face him. 'Do you mean what I think you mean?'

Helen gazed up at him. 'Do you mind?' she whispered and Milos's shout of triumph echoed across the moonlit water.

* * * * *

25

GREEK AFFAIRS: SLEEPING WITH A STRANGER

Anne Mather

First published in Great Britain 2005
by Mills & Boon, an imprint of Harlequin (UK) Limited,
Large Print edition 2012
Harlequin (UK) Limited,
Eton House, 18-24 Paradise Road, Richmond, Surrey TW9 1SR

© Anne Mather 2005

ISBN: 978 0 263 23625 5

Harlequin (UK) policy is to use papers that are natural, renewable and recyclable products and made from wood grown in sustainable forests. The logging and manufacturing process conform to the legal environmental regulations of the country of origin.

Printed and bound in Great Britain
by CPI Antony Rowe, Chippenham, Wiltshire